Unfolding
By Selena Kitt

eXcessica publishing

Unfolding © 2008 by Selena Kitt

All rights reserved under the International and Pan-American Copyright Conventions. No part of this book may be reproduced or transmitted in any form or by any means, electronic or mechanical, including photocopying, recording, or by any information storage and retrieval system, without permission in writing from the publisher.

This is a work of fiction. Names, places, characters and incidents are either the product of the author's imagination or are used fictitiously, and any resemblance to any actual persons, living or dead, organizations, events or locales is entirely coincidental. All sexually active characters in this work are 18 years of age or older.

This book is for sale to ADULT AUDIENCES ONLY. It contains substantial sexually explicit scenes and graphic language which may be considered offensive by some readers. Please store your files where they cannot be access by minors.

Excessica LLC
P.O. Box 127
Alpena MI 49707

To order additional copies of this book, contact:
books@excessica.com
www.excessica.com

Cover art © 2011 Willsin Rowe
First Edition November 2008

Warning: the unauthorized reproduction or distribution of this copyrighted work is illegal. Criminal copyright infringement, including infringement without monetary gain, is investigated by the FBI and is punishable by up to 5 years in prison and a fine of $250,000.

Chapter One

It started in the shower.

The kids slept until it was light out, their internal clocks finely tuned to the sun, but Jack and I had to roll out of bed long before then. He always hit the snooze button at least twice, and I usually snuggled up to his broad, strong back until he rolled me over to reverse spoon and pulled my hips in to him so I could feel how hard he was for me. There wasn't a day on earth that Jack didn't wake up hard. It made me smile and wiggle back against him, all sleepy eyes and long limbs.

It was a very rare occasion when we had time for morning sex in our rush to get everything ready and everyone out the door on time. Still, he loved it when I reached back and squeezed and tugged on him in those drifting moments still caught between sleeping and awake. I liked to imagine what he'd been dreaming about as I reached back to stroke him against my ass—what new flavor of the feminine had entered his unconscious during the night—a dark, exotic beauty; a long, slender blonde, some cool drink of water; or maybe a curvy, fiery redhead like me?

It was an awkward angle for me to do for very long, and sometimes he took his cock in his hand and rubbed it up and down the crack of my ass, or just moved the head against the soft skin of my cheek. Once in a while, if I'd forgotten and worn panties to bed, I'd curl my arm behind my back and pull my panties up tight. He loved to see me "bound" that way, even just the suggestion, my wrist twisted in the material and resting against my lower back, my bikini panties pulled taut and thin as a thong between my cheeks.

There were mornings when he felt more urgent, when he grabbed my hips and shoved his cock between my ass cheeks, rubbing it there, hard. Those mornings he'd press into me and stroke his cock against my ass, his breath coming faster against my neck, his cock an iron bar, hand pistoning up and down his shaft. I loved listening to the sweet flesh music of his hand on his cock. It made me moan and wiggle against him as I reached back to spread my ass for him—god, he loved that!—and arch my back so he could aim his cock at the tender little rosebud of my asshole. That usually sent him over the edge, my hands opening myself to him that way, and he would grunt and thrust and spill his cum deep into the crack of my ass.

Those were the days I really needed a shower.

I was the queen of fast showers, with a litany of things to do that day already running through my head. He was a shower lingerer, just standing for long moments under the water, soap in hand, while I was all-business, scrubbing and rinsing and shaving in record time.

Sometimes he could get me to linger with him, distract me from the endless lists of stuff to accomplish in my head. That's where it really started, although I recognize it now as a progression from our early morning ass-stroking sessions. It happened more on mornings when he was still excited, those mornings he didn't masturbate to completion in our bed, those mornings when his cock revived the minute soap and water were applied.

Those mornings he would take my hand and put it on his cock as he washed it, slick and hard and throbbing, something he knew never failed to interest me. I couldn't often resist a hard cock thrusting into my hand, even when there were other things to do.

Still, I would protest. "Jack, we can't. I forgot to make lunches last night."

"How about a little breakfast first?" He'd kiss me and then rub his fingers over my lips and I would know immediately what he wanted.

I loved sucking him off in the shower, although I didn't often get the opportunity. I loved kneeling in the needling spray, gulping down his cock and his cum, nearly drowning in the cascade of water over my head as he shoved himself into my mouth. My pussy got wet just thinking about it.

"Jack, we can't, really," I'd tell him, finishing rinsing my hair.

"Then just let me stroke myself against your ass."

And that's how it started, me bent over in the shower, my hands braced against the tile, my legs spread, the hot water running over my ass as he kneaded my flesh, spreading my cheeks open and rubbing his cock up and down my slit, teasing my pussy and my clit, before he began stroking himself right against my asshole.

But it didn't end there. Oh, no. That's just where it started. One morning, he put his finger there, a gentle probing, a tickling tease. I shied away at first, embarrassed. For me, there was a grave difference between his cock, too enormous to gain purchase against that tiny hole when he stroked it there, and his finger, which seemed to have a sly intention. Of course, I was right.

His finger, slippery with the soap he was using to lubricate his cock, slid into my asshole. When I hissed at him and told him no, he didn't take it out. Instead, he slid in another, increasing the pressure.

"Shh, Charlie, it's okay," he murmured to me, using the diminutive form of my name as a comfort measure as his fingers moved, slow, in and out.

"Jack!" I squealed as his fingers moved a little deeper. My face was flushed, and not just from the heat of the water in the shower. "That's...that's nasty!"

He chuckled, sliding his other hand between my legs, teasing my clit with one finger just the way he knew I loved. I moaned and arched my back, forgetting about what he was doing in my asshole for the moment.

"Does it feel nasty?" he asked me, rubbing my clit and fucking—yes, he was fucking my asshole—in a slow, easy motion and I was caught wiggling between shame and pleasure.

That first time, shame won out. I pulled away from him and got right out of the shower, drying off and not answering his calls, even when he stuck his head around the curtain.

When we talked about it later that night, as we were falling asleep, I blushed red again, telling him I didn't want to do anything like it, and that if he insisted on pushing it, we could just shower alone—but the threat sounded hollow, even to me.

And it was. It was only a week or so before he did it again, slipping his finger into my asshole as I was bent over in the shower. This time he'd waited, getting me fully aroused before beginning his gentle inquiry. That time, I didn't get out of the shower, and he came all over me with his fingers buried deep inside my ass.

The next time, I came so hard my ears were ringing, rubbing my own clit as he fingered my ass and pussy all at once. That time I turned around and sucked him off, as eager to have his cum as he was to give it to me.

The time after that, we crossed into entirely new and frightening territory. I was used to his fingers now, two, sometimes three of them fucking me at once. I liked rocking against him as he fingered my pussy and my ass together, filling me completely.

When he pressed the head of his cock against the tight ring of my asshole, however, that's where I drew the line. Again, I hurried out of the shower right away, dried off and ignored him for the rest of the morning, no matter what he said. It wasn't until late that night, the darkness providing enough cover for my shame, that I told him how scared I was, and he held me and rocked me and told me how much he loved me.

And that's how I got here—my ass in the air, my cheek resting against the cool sheet, two bottles of K-Y on the bed and Jack kneeling behind me, his cock slick and aimed toward a place I never would have believed I could let him enter.

"Wait, wait, wait!" My hands pressed his thighs, my eyes closed tight. The head of his cock was positioned *right there*. I was tense and couldn't seem to let go.

"It's okay, baby." He just rubbed me there, a familiar feeling. I let myself relax a little, enjoying the feel of his KY-slick fingers stroking my tender flesh.

"Okay, okay." I arched my back, taking a deep breath. I felt him press the head of his cock there again. The tip of him was easy at first as it met my soft, puckered opening, but then his engorged flesh stiffened and strengthened, coming up against a tight band of resistance. "Ohhhh wait, wait!"

He stopped, but he didn't pull back this time. I felt my own refusal, my whole body a bright red, flashing neon "No!"

"Play with yourself." His hands gripped my hips, cock pressed tight against my asshole. He wasn't giving up an inch now.

I reached between my legs, my fingers parting my lips. In spite of my fear, my pussy was swollen, wet, my fingers sliding easily among the delicate folds.

"God, you have such a beautiful cunt." His voice was full of lust and I knew he was watching me finger myself. I circled my clit with my index finger, large circles growing smaller, zeroing in at a slow, steady pace. A familiar tingling began between my legs and I lost myself in the sensation, working my fingers faster now, my breath hot against the sheet.

Jack pushed in a little further and I gasped and moaned. "Ohhhh no, honey! Wait, wait, please!" I begged him.

"Don't stop touching yourself." He pushed in a little harder.

I writhed beneath him. "Ohhh baby, honey, god, I can't take it! I can't take that much, please!" His cock felt three times its normal size. I felt my body rejecting him, wanting to expel him, find a way out of this. "Ohh Jack, oh my god, please!"

"It's okay." He was panting, as if what he was doing required a great deal of effort. I didn't know if it was the holding back or the pushing in. "Keep rubbing your clit."

I did, my fingers a sweet distraction from the hot throbbing steel rod pressing into my behind. "Oh please, please, please, please, please." I was begging him, and I didn't even know what for. Some sort of release?

"Just a little more," he whispered and I felt a slight pop as my ass opened to accept the entire head of his cock.

"Ahhhh god!" I was shaking, my face flushed. "No more, I can't!"

"That was the hardest part." His hands stroked my ass, my hips.

My body began to adjust to the feeling of his cock stretching me open in places it wasn't used to being distended. "Go slow. Please. Slow."

"Okay." His voice was a whisper, and he pulled on my hips, giving himself some leverage.

"Slow, slow, slow!" I felt him pressing deeper into me—the thin, tight band of flesh that had kept him at bay had now been pushed past, over the swell of him. He had a straight shot toward my center now.

"Jack, ohhhh god, it's so much!" I couldn't believe how vast he felt in me.

"Can you take more?" He squeezed my hips, his hands holding me steady.

"Yes." I breathed it into the bed. "Yes. Go ahead." He got himself another inch, maybe two. "Wait, wait!"

"Does it hurt?"

I shook my head, panting with the effort to take him into me. "No. I just... I have to get used to feeling it. So full."

"More?" His hips rocked a little.

"Yes." I pressed back against him, aching to feel the saddle of his hips against my ass. "Come on, that's it. Deeper. Is there more? Yeahhh, I can take it, baby. All the way in me."

Jack moaned as he sank into my flesh, buried now, to the hilt.

"You're in my ass." I was filled with wonder. "Oh my god."

"I'm gonna fuck your ass." His voice sent a shiver through me.

"Oh, honey, easy!" My mind had only just gotten wrapped around the idea of penetration—I hadn't made it to the idea of being fucked yet.

The delicate flesh around my asshole flowered open as he began to pull back, easing almost all the way out of me. I felt the tip of him, the ridge which had felt so impossible, easing out, and then back in.

"Slowwwww." My thighs shook. "Ohh honey, please, please."

He was moving now, in and out of my ass. "Oh, it's so tight. Charlie your ass is so tight!"

"Do you like it?" I pressed back against him, feeling how hard he was inside of me. "Do you like fucking my ass?"

He groaned, driving harder against me, and I met his thrust, rocking back. I loved the feel of him grinding into me, the sound of his grunts and moans. His lust, his pleasure, sent me soaring, and my fingers moving faster and faster over my clit.

"Harder," I whimpered, my fingers wet and slick with my juices as I circled my clit. "Ohh, please, fuck me harder!"

He did, his balls slapping against my pussy, his fingers using the bones of my pelvis like handle grips, pulling me back to him again and again. I loved feeling him ram into me with such force, with a slick, wild abandon that left me panting and moaning.

"Oh, fuck my ass!" I felt my orgasm building, his cock a driving force against my ass, my fingers working my clit for all I was worth. "I want you to come in my ass!"

He groaned at the words, and I felt him beginning to let go, his movements filled with purpose and longing now, heading toward an ecstatic finish line.

"Oooo baby, you're gonna make me come!" I arched my back and buried my fingers in my pussy as I shuddered with it, my thumb still rubbing on my clit, sending sweet waves through my body as I bucked and writhed beneath him.

He was just behind me, sliding me forward onto the bed, my knees collapsing as he plunged into my ass with all of his weight. His whole body quivered against the length of mine, his cock a throbbing wet pulse as he spilled waves of his cum into my depths.

When I was later tucked against him, my bottom still throbbing, I didn't wonder anymore how I got there as he petted me and held me and kissed my forehead, still flushed and sweat-dampened. For once, I didn't feel rushed or out of time. As I looked back at our journey toward that moment, I knew just how I got there—and I was filled with him and felt complete.

Chapter Two

By the time Jack and I crawled into bed, most nights all we wanted to do was sleep. He worked so hard, three jobs—well, two and a half—and between the kids and my job and the housework, I felt like I had three jobs, myself.

Sex became like an afterthought when we got so occupied with the daily rhythm of life. There were nights when I was very willing, but my body ended up in a tug-o-war between lust and exhaustion until I slipped off into sleep with my legs entwined with his, our breath the only thing mingling in the darkness.

Lately, though, I felt like some young teenager when it came to sex. I couldn't get enough, and I wasn't sure I could explain it. If someone in my past had ever told me one day I would be begging my husband to put his cock in my ass, I would have laughed until I peed my pants.

Yet, that's just what I found myself doing.

I'd joked that we should buy stock in K-Y—we had two tubes in both night table drawers and one in both bathrooms. I even put one in the living room end table drawer under a bunch of old copies of Reader's Digest after the time I ended up bent over the coffee table and one of us had to run back to the closest bathroom to get the K-Y.

Of course, Jack wasn't complaining. He was always up for sex, it seemed, even if he was tired. I didn't know how guys did that. He was very willing to comply with my requests—and I'd been requesting a lot.

In fact, I'd been craving it so much I got worried and started asking my friend, Jody, about how often she and her husband had sex—and if that sex might include something other than the usual?

I probably shouldn't have. The gist of our conversation gave me the impression that the only women who did anal sex did it for their husbands' sakes, and 'normal' women didn't really get any pleasure from it. So why did I find myself with my bottom in the air, begging Jack to put his cock in my ass more often than not?

I didn't know that I could quite describe my desire for it—or even justify it—as if that was really necessary. It turned Jack on and it turned me on. That should have been more than enough to make it acceptable. I felt so strange, wanting it, but I was compelled. I'd spent a lot of time trying to figure out what it was that appealed to me about it.

My friend, Jody, said, "That's an 'exit only' hole, baby!" That perked me right up. Maybe that was part of it? It was something so taboo, a "not supposed to." In that sense, it was a rebellion, right? So, what was I rebelling against? I asked Jack if he thought I was a rebel and he laughed. Pretty telling. Was that it, then?

The other night, after I had tucked the little ones in and finished the dinner dishes, I went and took a bath. Jack was in the living room on his laptop, trying to get some work done at home. I soaked in the tub and drifted, thinking about his cock in my ass.

What was it that made me want it so much? My pussy ached at the thought. I fingered my clit, back and forth, remembering him fucking me, hard and deep. It wasn't the heat of the water making me so flushed—it was remembering how he pounded me, made me beg, scream, come...

I wanted his cock in my ass. My finger on my clit wasn't anywhere near enough. I couldn't deny it. When I came out of the bathroom, I was wearing nothing but a little smile. It seemed to get his attention.

When I went over to the end table and dug under the Reader's Digests for the K-Y, his eyes brightened. I tossed the white tube on the coffee table, put a couch cushion on the floor, and knelt on it. Without a word, I went to my hands and knees and presented my ass to him. I heard him whistle, long and low, but I didn't move.

My breath came fast and shallow. My ass up in the air felt cool and it was tingling. I heard him closing his laptop, moving it aside, standing. Still, I waited, feeling that tingling spreading through my pelvis. I felt dizzy and weak when I heard him unzipping his pants.

"Spread your ass open for me." His voice was low. Commanding. I reached both hands back, going down to the floor on my shoulders, and opened myself to him, using my fingers to spread my cheeks as wide as I could. He groaned, and I heard the sound of his hand stroking his cock. I didn't look, though. I just kept my eyes closed, waiting.

I let out a satisfied sigh when he knelt between my thighs. His hands pushed mine away, kneading the flesh of my ass, opening and closing my cheeks, making my little asshole wink at him. I could imagine the lust in his eyes and it made my toes curl. My pussy was a throbbing mound of heat.

"What do you want?" he asked, using his finger to slide along my slit. I was already wet.

"Your cock," I murmured. This was a game we had started to play ever since he'd caught on to how much I loved his cock in my ass, and it made my breath come even faster.

"Where?" He rubbed my clit, making me shiver, and slid a finger inside of my pussy. "Here?"

"No." My voice was just above a whisper. I couldn't help rocking my hips against his hand, squeezing my pussy muscles around him.

"Where?" he asked. I moaned when I felt him touch my asshole with the tip of his finger, probing just a little. "Here?"

"Yes!" I hissed, wiggling back, arching.

"Are you sure?" I could hear his smile.

His fingers spread my pussy lips, and I knew I was wet enough for the curly red hair between my legs to be glistening with my juices. I felt his breath as he kissed my thighs, my ass.

"Are you sure you wouldn't rather have my tongue?" He slipped it into my slit. I groaned, feeling him sucking gently at my clit. It pulsed between his lips, a swollen, tender thing. He knew just what I liked, licking me in wide, flat sweeps now, again and again, making me gasp.

"Jack, please," I begged. I was yearning for him inside of me, filling me.

"Are you sure?" he murmured, teasing me, before he stuck his tongue deep into my pussy. I moaned, feeling his nose pressed against my little asshole. God, that felt good!

"Here," I whispered, pressing my flushed cheek to the carpet as I reached my finger around to show him, gently stroking my asshole. "Please."

"Mmm." The hum of his lips against my pussy made me shiver. I knew he was watching me rub my pink, puckered hole.

"Here?"

I jumped when I felt his tongue slip up to replace my finger.

"Jack!" I gasped. He grabbed my hips to keep me from moving away, licking my asshole in little circles. I groaned, hiding my face in my arms. Considering my current enthusiasm, I'd managed to get past most of the shame and my own prudence when it came to having his cock in my ass—but his *tongue?*

"Jack, don't," I whispered, but even as I said it, I arched my back for more. God, *his tongue!* He was just licking the sensitive, furrowed skin there, round and round the hole. The sensation made me weak and dazed with lust. My clit responded, even though his tongue pressed into my ass, as if it were being licked, too. I could feel the wet heat of his saliva dripping between my pussy lips.

"Do you really want me to stop?" he paused to ask, his thumb finding my aching clit. I shuddered, letting out a deep sigh.

"No." I felt my cheeks flush at my admission. He chuckled, but he put his mouth back there, more eager now, using the flat of his tongue, wiggling it back and forth over the soft crease. I groaned, rocking a little, my nipples grazing the carpet. His thumb on my clit never stopped either, rubbing in steady circles.

"God!" I cried when he made his tongue stiff, probing a little into my ass. Then he was lapping at me, again and again, faster and faster. His tongue was relentless, licking over and over that wrinkled little orifice, sending delicious waves of pleasure coursing through me.

"Baby, you're gonna make me come," I warned, but it just made him work faster, thumb rubbing, tongue licking, the sounds of encouragement in his throat sending me closer and closer to the edge. I tried, wanting the sensation to last forever, but I couldn't hold back. I shuddered against him, moaning loud and long, my toes curling as I came, writhing and convulsing on the living room floor.

"Don't move." His hands on my hips, holding me, sensing my desire to collapse. I didn't, managing to stay up on my knees, the world of light and sound fading in and out now with the beat of my pulse.

Out of the corner of my eye, I saw him grab the tube of K-Y off the table, and then I heard the slick sound of him stroking his cock with some. That made me groan, imagining his hand shuttling along the stiff length of him.

He squeezed some K-Y against my asshole. Oooo!—so cold compared to the warm wetness of his tongue. That I even had that frame of reference now made me flush again. He used his finger to work it, slow and easy, around that softly grooved passage, and then pressed it inside. I could tell when he switched from one finger to two, knowing the sensation of being stretched further and accommodating just a little more flesh.

I waited, patient, while he twisted and turned his fingers in me, probing deeper into that humid cleft, and then deeper still, until I was taking them completely.

"What do you want?" he asked again, and I smiled when I felt the head of his cock resting, throbbing, against the flexed, dimpled hole of my ass.

"Your cock," I whispered, my eyes still closed, lost in my own anticipation.

"Where?"

"My ass." I squeezed the very tip of his cock, trying to capture it with that winking, crinkled hole. "I want your cock in my ass."

He groaned then, and I felt him adjusting his position behind me for leverage, grabbing my hips as he pressed slowly in. I was used to this now, and knew just what to expect. I breathed deeper, down into my belly. My ass was tight, even after weeks of being fucked like this, and I still had to work to relax everything my pelvic region, knowing it made it so much easier for him to get in.

My ass never gave any indication that it wanted him. My pussy, on the other hand, was always accommodating, trying to suck him right in the minute he presented himself at entrance. My ass stayed clenched, like a pursed pair of lips refusing a bite of something bitter. I could never just receive him, the way I did when he slid inside my pussy. I had to consciously work at surrendering to the force of his cock.

"Wait," I whispered, feeling the maximum stretch now, the head of him spreading me open, seeking full entrance. It took so much trust for me to let him into the deepest, most secret parts of me. And yet, I wanted it like I'd never wanted anything else. I wanted his cock to probe those unseen depths, to open me beyond where I thought I could ever be opened.

"Okay," I breathed, and he pressed in again, responding to me, my movements, my voice, my noises. We both groaned when he slid his cock head past that tight ring of sphincter muscle, knowing I'd really given it up now. I was his—now it was just a matter of time.

He slid the length steadily inward, and I marveled at how huge he felt, how that tiny hole stretched to accommodate him. I had knelt in the tub several times these past few weeks, putting my own finger there, feeling its tightness and how different from my pussy it really was, awed by my own ability to open to him.

And I was opening, more and more, as he began to slide in and out, going easy with me. At first the sensation was centered at the place of greatest expansion—that constricted ring of muscle hugging his cock—but as he moved, and things began to loosen up, I became aware of him inside of me, plunging further and further into my depths.

"Okay?" Jack gasped, and I heard the pleasure in his voice.

What was it like to have something so tightly constricted, a band of heated muscle, sliding up and down the length of your cock? The difference in our experience was highlighted again for me in that moment, as I reached for the aching bud of my clit, rubbing it in easy circles. Between Jack's saliva, the KY and my own juices, I was literally soaking wet and my pussy made a sweet, wet noise as I touched myself.

"More," I murmured, giving him my assent. I had learned, I didn't just like my ass fucked—I liked it fucked *hard*—the harder the better.

He grabbed my hips and thrust himself into my center, making me moan and circle my throbbing clit faster. When he went deep like this, his cock rubbed some secret place buried deep in me. When he rocked there, it was like scratching some urgent itch I didn't even know I'd had.

"Harder," I gasped, reaching my other hand back for his hip, his thigh, wanting to shove him into me.

Sensing my eagerness, he grabbed my ass and began using all of his weight to drive into me, half-strokes, rubbing against that spot again and again. I didn't know if he knew about it—I had never told him—but he seemed attuned to my responses whenever he fucked me like this.

"Oh god," I moaned, the momentum of our fucking pushing me slowly off the cushion under me. I would have rug burn on my knees for a week. He was driving me forward, slapping into me, using his leverage to push in deeper than I thought possible, grunting with every motion.

"Oh fuck! Don't stop!" I cried, my fingers moving like lightning against my clit, feeling that delicious pressure inside of me building.

"I can't," he replied with a groan, and that made me moan, too, feeling his cock like a steel rod, coring me to a searing hot depth that went far deeper than my own belly. My pussy was quivering, on the verge, but my ass was on fire—a feverish, clutching tunnel of muscle pushing at him even as he drove inward.

"Fuck!" I screamed, not caring about the kids or anyone hearing, lost in the sensation of being filled completely. Jack was sweating and so was I, the wet slap of us together the only persistent sound in the room as he fucked me and fucked me until I was gasping and begging and biting my own arm to keep from screaming any more.

"Oh baby," I moaned, arching my back to urge him in at just the right angle. "Oh god, oh god, oh baby, god!" I'm not a religious person, and I don't know if there is a God, but I think I felt him in that moment, when the sensations in my pussy and my ass met and converged into one humming vibration—and then burst, like a delicious stream, flowing out in a rippling, pulsing gush, like I had become the heartbeat of the world.

Jack growled and swore, too, piercing me to my core with his last thrust. I felt the swell of him as he came, the endless waves surging along the underside of his cock, right past the tight band of muscle still hugging his shaft, and spilling into my ass, filling my deepest recesses with white hot fluid.

I groaned when he slid his cock out of me, at the tenderness of my flesh, and the aching hole he left when he went. He collapsed beside me on the floor, gasping for breath, looking at me through half-closed eyes. It took him somewhere, too, I thought. I didn't know if it was the same place—but I knew I loved going there.

"I need another bath," I murmured, resting my flushed cheek against my arm as I looked at him.

He smiled. "Yeah, let's get all clean again, so I can lick your little asshole some more."

I flushed, closing my eyes. What was it that I loved so much about being touched there? In the transition from passion to composure, I found myself wondering, curious, and more than a little awed by my own need.

I didn't know what it was.

But I realized I could analyze it from now until the end of time, and I still might never know. The only thing that I could really know was... I wanted it.

I gave Jack a dreamy smile as my ass quivered and I felt his cum slipping down my slit, knowing I didn't want to think about it anymore.

I just wanted to feel it, stiff and throbbing and filling me, taking me to places I had once only imagined. That was enough. More than enough.

Chapter Three

When Jack said, "We're taking a vacation," I just stared at him like he had three heads. Vacation? What was that? We hadn't taken time off or gone anywhere alone since before the kids were born. Who would take care of the house, the dog, the kids, water the plants, how would we get time off work?

"Tomorrow," Jack said, hiding a grin behind his coffee mug.

I turned from the dishwasher, standing there dripping water from a plate onto the floor, open-mouthed.

"It's all arranged," he said. "We're not going far. Friday through Sunday, so we don't have to take time off work."

"The kids—" I started, but he shook his head, really grinning now.

"All handled, I told you." His eyes were shining. "All you need to do is pack."

I put the plate in the dishwasher, grabbing a towel to wipe up the floor, absorbing everything he'd said. It wasn't like Jack to be spontaneous or cryptic. I was both excited and anxious, and when I looked up from the floor, he was still grinning.

"What kind of weather do I pack for?" I asked faintly.

Standing, he stretched and winked at me. "If I were you, I'd pack a lot of underwear."

I felt a heat creeping through my chest as his dark eyes met mine and I fully understood his meaning.

He turned to go out to the living room and said over his shoulder, "Oh, there's a little present for you upstairs on the bed."

It was in a huge round black velvet-covered box—almost like a hat box—except what I found inside weren't hats. There were four different panty and bra sets—black, red, white and pink. There were also thigh-highs to match, including a pair of black fishnets that caught my eye and made my breath catch. *So this is what he meant by underwear.* There was also a pair of black, four inch high heels.

The real surprise was at the bottom of the box—a clear gel-like rabbit vibrator, a glass/latex butt plug, and five tubes of K-Y. *Five!* I sat on the bed, pressing my hands to my cheeks to cool them. My pussy twinged and my ass clenched. Now I knew why it didn't matter where we were going, or that we weren't going far. We were obviously not going to leave the room very much!

* * * *

I didn't carry the velvet hatbox into the hotel. I packed everything into my rolling bag, including the new toys and the KY—I was careful to seal those in two Ziploc bags, just in case! I was wearing an outfit Jack had requested before we left, a white t-shirt and a black skirt that didn't quite come my knees—no bra, no stockings and no panties.

Rolling my bag behind me, I felt completely naked, my four inch heels clicking on the tile as we paused to check in. I felt a little like Julia Roberts in *Pretty Woman*, minus the blonde Cleopatra wig, as I followed Jack in his suit up to the counter. I couldn't count the looks I'd gotten on the way in, and it was only about seventy feet from the valet to the desk.

"Here you are, Mr. Thompson." The young clerk handed Jack two pass cards. His eyes were on my chest, and I knew my nipples were hard after coming in from the heat into the air conditioning. "I hope you and your lovely wife have a nice stay."

I smiled, flushing. "Thanks."

Jack slipped his arm around my waist, steering me toward the elevators. Upstairs, he told me to go into the bathroom and change.

"What color?" I smiled, rolling my bag behind me.

He sat on the bed, contemplating. "Come here." He crooked his finger at me.

I walked over to the bed, still getting used to the height of the heels, and stopped in front of him. Pulling me between his thighs, his hands ran up the smooth, bare skin of my legs, under my skirt, squeezing my ass.

"Ready for your vacation?" he murmured, resting his chin on my belly and looking up at me.

"I'm not sure." I bit my lip. "I still don't know what you have in mind."

He smiled. "I'm going to fuck you until you can't walk out that door. They'll have to bring in an ambulance with an IV just to re-hydrate you."

"Really?" I gasped, feeling his fingers working between my pussy lips, seeking the moist heat there.

"But I'm not just going to fuck this pretty little cunt," he murmured, slipping his fingers inside and forcing my thighs a little further apart. I gasped and wiggled, feeling speared on his hand between my legs. Then, he moved his fingers, dragging the wetness with him through the crack of my ass.

"I'm going to fuck this hot, tight little asshole," he growled, searching for and finding that soft, humid crease, sliding one finger into my ass, making me moan. "We're going to use every bottle of KY that we brought and have to go buy more."

"Are you ready for that?" His finger moved in and out of my ass, up to the first knuckle, his eyes on mine. I nodded, gasping, clenching my ass and squeezing his finger.

"Yes," I moaned, spreading my legs as wide as my skirt would allow.

"Good," he said with a grin and I groaned when he slid his finger out. "Go get changed. Black bra, white panties, black fishnets, and the shoes."

I stumbled back, catching myself on one of the dressers and grabbing the handle of my bag, rolling it with me into the bathroom. My hands trembled as I pulled out the clothes he requested, wondering at it. The panties were just white cotton with a lace edging and a little satin bow on the front. The bra, however, was a black lace thing that just screamed "whore."

It seemed a strange combination, but I put it all on, glancing at myself in the mirror over the sink. It was a three-way thing, and I could see myself from every angle as I turned, red curls falling around my flushed cheeks as I made my adjustments.

When I came out of the bedroom, he was naked on the bed, a few pillows tucked behind his head. His eyes lit up when he saw me and he let out a low whistle.

"Where's the KY?" he asked.

I smiled, bringing the bag out from behind my back. I was more than ready. I tossed it toward him and he caught it, opening the Ziploc bag and fishing out the tubes.

He threw one back at me. "For the bathroom. Leave it on the counter."

I walked back to the bathroom, still just a little unsteady in the heels, peeking around the corner to put the KY next to the sink. When I turned back, Jack was pacing, tossing pillows around the room. He threw a bottle of KY next to the two pillows on the floor, one on each side of the bed. He put one on each night table.

"What are you doing?" I asked, putting my hands on my hips and cocking my head at him.

"Tactical maneuvers," he murmured, looking over at me with a grin. "Reinforcing my supply lines."

I laughed, shaking my head. He sat on the bed, crooking his finger at me again, and with a sense of deja-vu, I came to stand between his thighs. His hands moved over my hips in the white cotton panties and then slid up to my breasts in the black lace bra, pushing my flesh up until it threatened to spill over the top.

"Angel and slut." His breath moved hot against my belly as he kissed me there, and I finally understood his choice in garments. His thumbs rolled over my nipples through the lace and I sighed, arching my back toward him. He licked them through the fabric, making fat circles around and around.

Slipping my hand through his hair, I pulled him closer, moving forward and sitting on his leg, rubbing my pussy over his thigh. I'd been wearing the panties less than five minutes and they were already damp. His cock was hard, brushing against the lace top of my thigh high as I ground my hips against him—the heat of it was incredible.

Reaching down, I tugged on his shaft, rubbing my thumb over the tip, making him groan against my breasts with his face buried there. Slowly, I slid down his thigh, kneeling between his legs and looking up at him. His cock pointed straight at my mouth, as if it knew just what it wanted, and I reached my tongue out for it, licking all around the tip, making it wet.

Jack made a happy noise in his throat, looking down to see himself disappearing into my mouth. I loved sucking his cock, and I knew just what he liked, teasing and licking and even nibbling at first, just at the tip, until he started leaking pre-cum. Then I opened my mouth wide, taking him in as far as I could go, usually about halfway at first, working him deeper and deeper with every pass.

Putting my hands behind my back as I sucked him, I crossed my arms at the wrists. It was my version of "see, no hands!" and he loved it, grabbing my hair, growling and thrusting, using my mouth and throat for his pleasure. There were times when I could, and did, do this for hours, in various positions, bringing him to a near-boiling point again and again, only to back off for a while, licking his thighs, his balls, his belly, and then starting all over.

Today, though, he clearly had other things in mind, because he grabbed my hair, pulling my lips off his cock. It made a wet pop when it came out of my mouth, and I reached for his cock with my tongue, whimpering, still wanting that thick thrust in my throat.

"Hungry little slut," he murmured with a smile, taking his cock and rubbing it over my eager lips and tongue. "Is your pussy hungry, too?"

I moaned, nodding, touching the crotch of my panties. They weren't damp anymore—they were soaked.

"I know what else is hungry." He pulled me to standing. Still wearing the heels, I wavered a little as he stood, turning me and pushing me face forward onto the bed. He spread my thighs wider and then I could feel his hands on my ass, running over the white cotton panties, squeezing the firm, rounded globes of my cheeks.

"You've got a hungry little asshole, don't you, baby?" he whispered, and I moaned when he used his palms to spread my cheeks wide, the panties slipping between the crack. There was something so wicked about it. The shock of it was part of what made it so appealing.

"Oh, god!" I cried, feeling his mouth between my ass cheeks, through my panties, nosing and rutting and growling as he buried his face there. His chin dug into the crotch of my panties, rubbing against my pussy, and I felt his tongue lapping, making the already wet material even wetter, working over the delicate, grooved skin of my asshole.

"Up." He pulled on my hips until I was on my knees, my face buried in my arms. I still wasn't quite used to feeling his tongue against the sensitive flesh of my ass, and I found myself caught somewhere between shame and pleasure.

He tugged my panties down to my knees, his fingers moving through the soft, wiry red hair of my pussy, parting my lips. They were swollen open as if they were aching to be parted. My clit was hiding, pulled up high under its fleshy hood like it always did when I was very excited, as if it wanted to be teased out.

Jack found it, moving his fingers in soft, slow circles around, and I felt his breath on my thigh and my ass. I rocked back against him, down on my forearms on the bed, my breasts swaying and my nipples grazing the bedspread. He teased my clit for a while, feathering kisses over my bottom until I was moaning and trembling under his hands.

"Ready for your vacation?" Jack knelt up between my legs. He slid his cock between my lips, up and down, working the fat head through my flesh. I gasped when he shoved into me, my pussy opening easily, slippery wet, sucking him in.

He pumped into me a few times, his hands on my hips, moaning when I squeezed my muscles around the thick length of him.

"Gonna take you far, far away," he breathed, slipping his cock out and using it to slap my asshole. I jumped, whimpering, and he did it again, a hard, flat sound, the head of his cock thwapping against the wrinkled opening.

"Yes," I whispered, my body responding, Pavlovian, when I heard the sound of the KY tube snapping open. There was the slick sound of him pumping it over his cock, and then a cold daub between my cheeks. His fingers rubbed it over the furrowed skin there, round and round, but didn't slip inside.

"Can you take me?" He pressed the head of his cock against my flexed, puckered hole. I felt my body tense. He had never tried to slide into me without easing the way at least a little first, with a finger or two or three.

"I don't know," I admitted, my face still buried in my arms.

He used his fingers to press the spongy head of his cock into the tight, closed aperture of my ass. I took a deep breath, realizing I'd been holding it, knowing he would never get in if I didn't relax.

"Jack!" I moaned, my toes curling and my fists clenching as he pushed a little deeper into the grooved passageway, the head of his cock meeting that snug band of muscle inside. I felt it burning a little as it stretched taut and I bit my arm, closing my eyes tight.

"You can do it," he murmured, his hands stroking my ass, a tender caress.

He was demanding entrance, a thick steel heat throbbing as he nudged his way through a slowly relenting orifice. The winking eye of my asshole was stretched wide around his cock, and I realized I was taking him in, surrendering to the strain and force and weight of him as he pushed, inch by inch, into the dimpled cavity of my ass.

"There it is," he murmured as we both felt my asshole concede, submitting to him with a slick "pop," that hot band of muscle snug around his shaft now. I had acquiesced, waved the white flag—I was his.

But that was only the beginning. It was a long way from tip to base, the journey of a lifetime, inch by inch, step by step, and I moaned and writhed the whole way as he pushed his thick length deeper and deeper, seeking the darkest, most intimate parts of me as he did. And I gave them to him, bit by humbling bit, my skin stretched to screaming while my body ached to be filled.

When he was in, balls-deep and trembling, his fingers gripping my hips, I sighed as if he had just revealed something, a long-kept secret, and knew that now, I could fly. That's what it felt like when he began, my ass still pushing at him to "go!" even with the slick and slippery way we had made. It was against everything, it shouldn't have been possible, and yet it was. I could fly.

He started fucking me, pulling me back onto him while he pushed in, finding more room to move. I moaned when he changed angles, thrusting up for a while, and then in deep. He pressed my hips to the bed, my ass cradling him as he laid his full weight on me and thrust, leaving me breathless and trembling.

"Come here." He slid his cock out of my ass. I groaned, looking back at him in panic. I had never had him out of me and then back in again. Could I take him? He slid my hips back and back, until my knees were at the edge of the bed. He gave me a pillow to hold onto, and I did, as I heard the cap to the KY again, just in case.

He stood behind me, his cock poised and throbbing against my now gaping asshole. I felt how open it was for him, how he had made it yield. He slid back in without any effort, seeking a core depth I didn't think possible. He had more leverage now, standing behind me, and he drove into me hard, my body rocking with the shock of the motion.

"Oh god!" I wiggled my hand between my legs, finding my sopping pussy, my throbbing clit. He was a force of nature, the impact of his hips jolting me alive, sending hot tingling sparks up my spine. I felt everything—the way my asshole flexed and pushed at him, the fat swell of his cock as he fucked me, the bruising grip on my hips, the slow, spiral upward that was my climax.

I felt myself floating toward it, nearing an edge I knew I was going to sail over. He grunted and thrust into me, using his cock to impale me deeper, harder, the tip of him so lost in my dark tunnel I didn't know where we began or ended. I was whimpering, moaning, thrashing, rubbing my clit, making fast circles against my flesh.

"Jack!" I cried as he dug even deeper—fuck!—spearing me, driving me forward on the bed. I lost one of my shoes and it dropped to the floor with a thud as he sent me forward again, again, pulling me back with his hands on my hips, taking me and fucking me until I couldn't see straight, think straight—I was just his, lost in the sensation of us.

"Now we're getting there," he growled, giving me long, full strokes, tip to tail, grunting with every one.

"Yes, there," I moaned, my fingers finding the secret code, unlocking the sweet release buried somewhere under the bud of flesh between my thighs. "I'm there, oh Jack, I'm there!"

And I was, twisting and moaning at my peak, soaring off the edge and riding the swells as I came. My pussy contracted, a tight, fast flutter, but my ass pushed at him, "out, out!" and he groaned when that taut band of muscle ringed the head of his cock. He was there, too, and I felt him rolling with it, his hips bucking forward with the surge, white hot bursts deep into my belly, like flashing images in my mind, again and again.

When he eased himself out of me, I collapsed onto my belly on the bed, my white cotton panties around my knees, still wearing everything but the shoes. Jack climbed over me, sliding up next to me with a groan.

"Where are we?" I murmured, turning so I could snuggle up against him.

He smiled, his eyes still closed. "Does it matter?"

I touched my trembling palm to his and realized it didn't matter at all.

Chapter Four

"Jack, the door!" I went to stand up fully, unclasping my hands from where they were wrapped around my ankles.

"No!" He pressed my head back down until my nose nearly touched my shins. "Stay there. I ordered room service while you were in the bathroom."

"Jack!" I moaned, knowing when he opened the door, the waiter would see me jackknifed in front of the bed, wearing only a pair of black fishnets and four-inch heels, my ass filled with a clear butt plug and my pussy swollen and dripping wet underneath. I was just glad I could hide my red face behind my legs.

"Hi, bring it on in," Jack said, and the words made my heart lurch and my belly clench. My first instinct was to run, to cover myself, but I fought it, feeling even more blood fill my face.

The dishes on the tray clattered as the cart—and the person pushing it, I presumed—moved into the room. I was lightheaded enough already from being upside-down, but now I really felt faint.

"Thanks, we're starving," Jack remarked as the door swung closed. "What do I owe you?"

"Uh..." It was a male voice, young, and I closed my eyes, willing myself anywhere else but here. "W-we charge it to your room, sir."

"Good enough, then here's your tip." Jack was still wearing his jeans, but no shirt, and I heard him dig his wallet out of his back pocket.

"Th-thank you, sir. That's very generous of you." The young man's voice shook, and I wondered what he could possibly be thinking. Part of me really wanted to know, I discovered.

"No, thank *you*," Jack said. "We're working up quite an appetite."

"I can see that, sir," the young man replied, and I swear I could feel his eyes on me, looking at the glass butt plug spreading my ass wide open, allowing for a clear view inside, according to Jack. My pussy was soaking wet and throbbing.

"You like what you see?" Jack asked and I groaned softly, gripping my ankles tight.

"Uh..." There was a moment of quiet, and I couldn't contain my curiosity. I poked my head out around my legs, seeing a young man standing at the doorway. His eyes were round as saucers under a pair of wire-rimmed spectacles, making them look even larger, and he ran a hand through his short dark hair as he stared at me.

"You can say so," Jack replied, and I looked at him. He was smiling at me, his eyes bright. "She's something, isn't she?"

I couldn't believe he was doing this, and while my head screamed I should run to the bathroom and lock the door right this minute, my body seemed to be responding to this humiliation. A slow heat spread through my pelvis and my pussy ached.

"Y-yes, sir," the young man breathed, shifting from foot-to-foot.

Jack clapped him on the back, turning him with his big body. "Well, thanks again."

"You're welcome." I saw him glance over his shoulder as Jack propelled him out the door.

The young man was facing me, and he licked his lips, looking at Jack. "Leave the cart outside your door when you're finished. And if there's anything else you need... anything... just let me know. Ask for Lloyd when you call down, okay?"

"Will do." I heard Jack grinning as he shut the door.

"Jack!" I gasped, watching him walk toward me, the upside-down view making me dizzy. "What were you thinking?!"

He chuckled, coming up behind me and grasping my hips, rubbing denim against my skin, his zipper biting me as he pulled me roughly back, shoving the butt plug in to its maximum depth, making me fully aware of it again. His cock was hard—I felt it like an iron bar between us.

"What did you think of Lloyd?" His fingers kneaded the flesh of my ass, his hips rocking, pressing the butt plug rhythmically into me. "Or, better yet, what do you think Lloyd thought of you?"

"He probably thought I was a slut," I murmured, feeling his hand moving between us, searching for my pussy lips and finding them.

"Don't you like being a slut?" He slid two fingers into my pussy. "Don't you want to be my little slut?"

I moaned as he started moving his fingers, twisting them in my wetness. They made a wet sound as they moved in and out of me, faster and faster.

"Oh Jack!" I felt his thumb on my clit, finally, my whole body responding and beginning to quiver. "Yes!"

"Tell me." He pushed his fingers in deep and kept them there, his thumb strumming my clit, focused, practiced and precise. "Tell me you're my little slut."

"Yes!" Gasping, I arched my back, the sensation between my legs so intense I could barely breathe. "Yes, yes, I'm your little slut...your naughty, dirty little slut."

"That's my girl," he groaned, and I heard his zipper coming down. "Did you like Lloyd seeing you with your bare ass up in the air?"

His cock was out, pressing where his fingers had been, parting my lips.

"Oh god!" I cried, feeling him move forward, grabbing my hips and shoving himself hard into my pussy. I felt off-balance, reaching toward the floor to steady myself.

"Put your hands on your ankles," Jack instructed, his cock buried to the hilt, now, pushing the butt plug deep with his weight.

I did what he asked, gripping my ankles so tight the fishnets made criss-cross patterns on my palms. He was fucking me, pulling his cock out slow, nearly all the way out, before plunging back in, hard. I had never felt so completely filled.

"I think you liked it." He pulled me back into the saddle of his hips and kept me there. "Does it get you hot, knowing you made his cock hard? He's going to go find the nearest bathroom and jack off, you know, thinking about you bent over with this butt plug shoved into your tight little asshole."

I moaned as he twisted it in my ass, sending a shiver through me. The thought of that man—little more than a boy, really—jerking off and imagining me, made my knees weak. I might have collapsed if Jack hadn't been holding onto me so tight.

"He wanted to fuck you." Jack moved his cock in me again, short strokes. "He wanted to fuck your hot, wet little cunt, just like this."

"Oh, Jack," I moaned, my pussy on fire, my asshole spread around the shaft of the butt plug, stretched so tight I could barely stand it.

"Think you'd like that?"

He grabbed me, pulling me to fully stand and turning me around to face him. The world tilted, the blood pounding in my head, my face tingling as he kissed me, hard, plunging his tongue deep. I couldn't stay standing, and he sensed my collapse, gripping my arms and pressing me back onto the bed, spreading my thighs with his as he entered me again, fucking me while holding both of my wrists above my head.

"Does it feel good, both of those holes being filled?" he grunted into my ear, his cock driving in. I felt stretched open, the sensation beyond anything I'd imagined, as he pounded into me again and again. "Tell me, baby."

"Yes, yes," I gasped, my nails digging hard into his back. "Oh I love both of my hot, tight little holes being filled. Fuck me hard, Jack, make me cum for you!"

He groaned, thrusting deeper, faster, my whole body jolting with the impact, my pussy throbbing and aching for release. I was so close, panting, clutching him, fucking him back as much as I could, working toward my orgasm. When it came, I bit his shoulder, the spasms shuddering through me, my pussy squeezing the length of his cock and my asshole contracting, threatening to expel the butt plug, but he kept it pressed deep into me with his weight.

"Oh Jack," I whispered, breathless, as he pulled out of me, still hard and glistening with my juices. "Oh, god, that was so good."

"Hold your legs back," he instructed, his fingers gripping the wide end of the butt plug, wiggling it back and forth it my ass and making me squirm.

I grabbed my knees, watching as he slowly eased the clear, hard length out of my asshole, feeling every ridge as it slid out, slippery with K-Y, my muscles contracting, in a hurry to resume their proper shape. He set the butt plug up on the night table and opened the drawer, reaching in and pulling out the rabbit vibrator and another bottle of K-Y and setting them on the bed next to me.

"What are we going to do with that?" I looked up at him with wide-eyes.

"You'll find out." He slipped his jeans and shorts down his hips and then straddled me, moving his hard cock up towards my mouth. He pressed the head to my lips, rubbing it there, still slick with my juices. "Suck."

I took him in, rolling my tongue around the head and pulling the skin taut with my hand the way I knew he loved.

"Oh, yeah," he groaned as I sucked him deeper, using my other hand to grab his ass and pull him in, the muscles tight and hard.

His cock throbbed against my tongue, and I licked the taste of me off his shaft, all the way down to the base and back up again. The feel of him in my mouth made my pussy ache, and I longed for something, the throb between my legs incredible. After being so filled, I felt empty now, and wanted more.

I was eager, sucking him greedily, moving my head up and down his length, using my mouth like a tight, wet cunt, just a hot, wet channel for him to fuck. He groaned and grunted, thrusting over my tongue, hard into my throat, making me gag a little, but neither of us cared. I tasted his pre-cum and swallowed, loving the taste of us together.

"Okay, okay," Jack gasped, grabbing a handful of my hair and pulling me back, easing his cock out of my mouth. I reached my tongue out for him, using the tip to lick at the head, my eyes on his.

"Hungry little slut," he murmured, and I smiled as he slid between my thighs and grabbed the tube of K-Y.

I watched as he squirted some over the head of his cock, still wet from my mouth.

"Pull your legs back, again," he said, and I did, feeling him resting against my aching asshole. I hadn't realized how stretched I was from the butt plug until his cock touched that crinkled little hole.

"Oh god," I whispered, my nails digging to my knees as I pulled them back, feeling him pressing forward. It didn't matter that I had been stretched open for nearly half an hour, that tight band of muscle had managed to contract down again and was pursed against his entry.

"Easy," he murmured, one hand on my thigh, the other guiding his cock.

He shifted his weight, pressing in, and I gasped as the head of his cock sought entrance and slipped past the constriction, the puckered hole of my ass opening at his insistence. There was a familiar concession as he slid slowly into that dark, private orifice, and while I had to submit, allowing him access to my tight, dimpled flesh, it was a gentle acquiescence. The butt plug must have stretched me open more than I realized, because he'd never been able to slip in so easily before.

"Ready?" He leaned into me, the length of his cock moving to search my depths.

I sighed, closing my eyes as he made his way in, much faster than ever before, until I felt his pelvis pressed tight against my ass. He started sliding back out, my flesh relieved, as it always was, at the thought of being free of the obstruction, but then he pressed back in again, making me moan. It was always such a shock, feeling the delicate flesh there giving in to him, buckling under his hard heat and weight as he made his way along that fissured passage.

I always felt so humbled in these moments, the heat of such an intimate, secret part of my body being opened and entered, the shame of it slowly being overridden by the wicked, carnal delight of it. We did that push-pull for a few moments, and he would stop when he was almost all the way out, rubbing his cock head against the tight ring there, the one that seemed to want to squeeze him right back out. He teased the hole with the ridge of his flesh, before pressing back into my dark recesses again. He did that until I was rocking under him, moaning and panting out loud.

"Feel good?" He slid his fingers through my pussy lips.

I nodded, my eyes half-closed, feeling myself being carried away. His thumb found my clit, moving in circles, making me moan. He'd never had such easy access before, and it surprised me, how open and exposed I was to him, his cock buried in my ass as he rubbed my pussy.

"So tell me the truth." He watched my face as he fucked me, slow now, still teasing my asshole when he eased himself back. "Did you like Lloyd looking at you?"

I remembered the look of lust on the young man's face, the way his eyes moved over me, and I nodded, feeling a heat spreading through my cheeks.

"He wanted you." Jack slid two fingers into my pussy. "He wanted this wet little cunt. Think he'd ever seen anything shoved up a woman's ass before?"

"Oh!" I gasped as his fingers started moving in me, in and out, the same rhythm as his cock.

"I bet Lloyd would love to fuck your ass," he breathed, his eyes on mine. The thought made me breathless. "Would you like to feel his hard cock sliding into your tight little asshole, baby? See the look his face as he took a woman's ass for the first time?'

"Jack!" I gasped, squirming under him at the thought. It turned me on more than I was willing to admit.

"Lloyd could fuck your sweet ass," he went on, plunging his cock deep into that hot, constricted tunnel, making me moan. "And I could slide into to your pussy...would you like that, baby? Being filled by two cocks?"

"Oh god," I whispered, closing my eyes to it, my pussy throbbing with wanting. The fantasy had completely captured me.

The thought of being opened up and filled like that made me feel faint. I imagined that stunned young man—Lloyd—sliding his cock into my ass for the first time as I knelt on the bed over Jack. I would have to guide him, show him, reach underneath and use my own hand to press him past that tight resistance. Then to have Jack slide his cock into me, too! Oh god!

"Jack!" I felt something hard pressing against the entrance of my pussy and looked down to see him holding the vibrator.

"Let's see if you'd like it." He twisted the cock-like head around as he pressed it slowly in.

"Oh, wait!" I cried, the hard shaft beginning to fill me, opening me wide. It was already halfway in and I felt some sort of maximum stretch burning between my legs. I had to get used to it, the sensation so intense I felt like I was going to burst.

"I can feel it," he told me hoarsely, stopping for a moment, wiggling the vibrator, twisting it around. "There's just a thin layer of flesh between my cock and this one."

"Does it feel good?" I looked up at him with wide eyes.

He nodded, groaning, pressed it in deeper, making me gasp. I felt the head of it wanting to go further, and he eased it in, more and more, until it was buried inside of my pussy. I trembled, looking down at the little rabbit sitting on top of the shaft resting against my slit, his ears nudging my clit.

"Turn it on," I begged, and he did, the rabbit buzzing softly, making me moan and squirm. His cock jumped—I felt it in my ass, the muscles of that tight passage very sensitive to the rhythmic throb of his shaft.

"Can you feel that?" I watched his face as he turned the vibrator up even further, the hum sending shivers through me.

"Yeah," he gasped, pulling his cock slowly out and pressing it back in. "It's good."

I was stretched wide, my skin taut, but everything slippery wet and swollen as he started moving the cock inside of my pussy in time with his cock in my ass. His flesh was softer and had more give, more delicious heat, but the vibrator hummed, the little rabbit's buzz traveling up the hard shaft, deep inside of me.

"Oh god, look at that," I moaned, arching against him, curling around so I could watch myself get fucked by two cocks at once.

He smiled, wiggling his eyebrows, his gaze moving over my face. "Wait...there's more."

I cocked my head at him and then looked down between my legs, where he pressed a second button on the vibrator. Something came to life inside of my pussy, the shaft of the cock there making a rhythmic hum, and I remembered the rotating beads buried in the length of the dildo.

"Jack!" I gasped, collapsing back fully on the bed, my heels falling to the sheets, the points digging into the mattress so I could press back, up against him.

"Feel good?" He pushed the button, driving those beads around and around at the sensitive entrance of my pussy.

"Oh fuck!" I cried as he began moving everything at once, his cock like steel heat in my ass, the vibrator stimulating my clit and my cunt together, in and out in a rocking rhythm, making everything feel swollen and thick between my thighs.

"You're so tight like this!" His eyes closed as he started to fuck me, his cock not teasing anymore, but taking long, hard strokes as he shoved the vibrator deep into me.

He drove forward, leaning into me, shoving my thighs back as he took my ass, the cock buried in my cunt making us both moan with its steady hum. Jack growled and grunted as he slid into the tight, puckered heat of my asshole, pounding me so hard our flesh made a wet slapping sound as we came together again and again.

Lost in the pleasure of it, he grabbed my ankles and pressed my knees back practically to my ears and I slipped my hand between us, searching for the vibrator and fucking myself with it, wanting more, not just to be filled but to be fucked hard in both holes, completely taken. The only thing missing was something to fill my mouth, and I grabbed Jack's hand, taking his finger into my mouth and sucking hard.

Watching me, Jack moaned, thrusting even deeper, and I knew I wasn't going to last. I wanted to—I loved feeling filled, two hard cocks seeking the center of my flesh, buried to the hilt and exploring my depths. The heat in my belly was too much, the buzz between us a driving force, and I knew I was going to explode.

I sucked hard on the finger in my mouth, moaning and squirming under his weight, feeling the swell of my orgasm breaking over me, pushing the taut ache in my belly past the point of no return. My pussy contracted around the vibrator, the rabbit's slippery ears buzzing my clit into ecstasy, and my asshole spasmed tightly around Jack's slick length. I was carried away completely, moaning and whimpering as the pleasure shuddered through my body.

"Oh fuck!" he cried, feeling my ass clamping down on the head of his cock.

I knew he couldn't hold back and he shuddered, bucking his hips into me as he started to come, too. He strained against me as his cock erupted, spilling his hot cum in generous swells, exploding into the deep, humid cavity he thrust hard into again and again. There was so much I couldn't contain it, and I felt his cum slipping down the crack of my ass toward the bed as he shoved his length into me.

I groaned, sliding the buzzing vibrator out of my wetness and tossing it, still humming, onto the bed. Jack leaned over me, kissing my cheek, my ear, his cock softening slowly. It stayed in my ass, though, until he shifted his weight, pulling the length of it out. He rolled off me, propping himself up on his elbow.

"Hungry?" he asked, glancing over at the cart.

"Starving!"

"Good." He smiled, leaning over and biting playfully at my nipple, making me squeal. "Hope you're still in the mood when I call Lloyd to come get the cart."

I stared at his broad, strong back as he sat up, my heart racing. "Are you serious?"

"Maybe." He grinned at me and winked.

Chapter Five

"We're not going to leave this room at all, are we?" I murmured, feeling Jack's hand moving up from the back of my knee to my thigh under the covers. I couldn't remember the last time we'd taken a nap together in the middle of the afternoon, and the late-afternoon sun peeking through the heavy curtains felt decadent, a rich, sweet indulgence.

"That was my plan," he agreed, bridging the distance between us on the huge king-size bed. I smiled when his body met mine and he pulled me close, tucking my hips and bottom against him, snug and warm.

"What else do you have planned?" I bit my lip, moving my behind against his crotch. I couldn't remember the last time we had indulged in this much pleasure either, come to think of it.

"You're going to find out," he assured me, sliding his hand over the swell of my ass, his finger slipping between the crack. I gasped and wiggled when he found the sensitive flesh of my asshole, just rubbing there, around and around.

I felt as if my body had been keeping secrets, and now it was revealing just how much pleasure it was really capable of.

"But I will tell you," he went on, his breath tickling my ear, his finger probing the tiniest bit. "At the moment, my plans involve using that Jacuzzi tub over there."

"Easy," I whispered, liking his finger where it was and turning a little so he had more access. "I'm a little sore."

"Oh, poor thing..." He kissed my neck, licking at the spot that always made me shiver with pleasure. "A hot bath will do you a world of good, then..."

I stretched and gave a lazy yawn, blinking over at the vast, white tub in the corner of the room. It was very over-the-top, with huge white pillars on three corners from ceiling to its tile edge, which was covered with plants and greenery. At least it's not heart-shaped, I thought, and smiled, scooting off the bed with a look over my shoulder at Jack.

"You look positively wolfish." I glanced back to him as I bent and turned on the water. "What are you looking at?"

He was leaning up, watching me. "Your ass."

"One track mind." I shook my head as if in protest, turning back to adjust the water.

"Maybe...but you don't seem to mind." He pushed the sheet aside to reveal his hardening cock.

I pretended my flush was from the steam rising from the water. "So?"

"Show me." His hand squeezed, released, and I watched over my shoulder, feeling my breath catch as he slid the skin up over the tip and back down again.

I arched my back just slightly, my thighs a little more open, teasing. "What do you want to see?"

"Spread it open for me," he instructed, his eyes dark and focused.

Swallowing, I parted my thighs, tilting my bottom, giving him a view of my pussy. His hand moved a little faster when I reached between my legs and parted my flesh, showing him.

"Your ass, baby," he murmured, his eyes never leaving that spot. "Show me that little asshole."

Really flushing now, I reached back with one hand, balancing with the other on the edge of the tile, and showed him what he wanted to see.

"God," he groaned, his hand moving even faster. "That's so sweet. Use both hands."

I had to bend completely over to do it, resting my forehead against the edge of the tub, one hand on each cheek, pulling them apart to he could see it all. Standing there, completely exposed and vulnerable, my heart racing, I had never been so aroused. I could almost feel his eyes on me, sweeping up from my pussy lips to the dimpled hole of my ass.

"Sore, huh?" he asked, his voice right behind me, his finger trailing down the crack of my ass, making me jump.

"Only a little," I protested, feeling his cock, hard and insistent, pressed between my lips.

"Maybe we should give it a rest." He slid his cock slowly into my pussy, opening me, making me moan with the length and width of it spreading me wide. "What do you think?"

"Oh, Jack," I gasped when he grabbed my hips, pressing himself snugly inside, the head of his cock nuzzling itself against my womb. I squeezed myself around him and heard his sharp intake of breath, loving the way his hands gripped me harder.

"Maybe I should just fuck your tight little cunt?" he growled, beginning to move, and I grabbed the edge of the tub to keep my balance, groaning at his words. "Fuck you until you can't decide which is more sore..."

"Ohhhh, please," I moaned, lifting my hips, wanting him deeper still. His fingers gripped my ass tight, and then I felt his thumb strumming over the delicate opening of my asshole, sending little shivers through me.

"But I think you still want your ass fucked." His thumb pressed, making me gasp and squirm. "Don't you?"

I groaned again, flushing at the humiliation of it, the admission still too much. I knew he was going to make me say it, and just the anticipation made my pussy clench.

"Tell me." He moved his hands off my behind, his thumb gone from the tender hole of my ass. "Show me."

I knew what he wanted. Trembling, with his cock still moving slick, slow, in and out, I rested my forehead against the edge of the tub again, reaching back to open my cheeks, spreading them wide. He let out a long breath and his cock twitched inside of me, just the head of it pressing between my wet lips.

"You love it, don't you?" He slid the wet heat of his cock up to touch that puckered hole.

I squirmed and whimpered, "Yes..."

Just how much I loved it, I couldn't admit, even to myself. My ass tightened at the thought of being filled, teasing the tip of his cock with its clench.

"You'd better shut off the water." He moved around me to step into the tub.

Dizzy, I let out a pent-up breath, reaching for the nozzles and turning them both as Jack sank down and turned on the jets. The water bubbled and foamed and my eyes met his as I slid my legs over the side into the heat.

I groaned when I sank in beside him, the water enveloping and buoying me at once. His hands met my waist, slipping down my hips and pulling me toward him as we kissed, the steam beginning to rise between us. I found his cock with my hand, pulling and tugging it against my belly as we rocked, his tongue doing things to my mouth my body had forgotten, sending electric pulses straight to my core.

Rubbing him up and down my slit, I couldn't stand it anymore and I sank down onto his hardness, wiggling my bottom and wrapping my legs around him. He held me close, using his weight to press me up, the water making waves around us as we fucked. When his thumb found my clit, I whimpered, opening my eyes for only a moment before sinking again, lost in the sweet sensation.

"So close," I whispered into his ear, biting the lobe, gnawing at his neck. My nails dug hard into the wet flesh of his back, but he didn't notice, his breath coming faster. My words spurred him on, and his other hand slid around behind me as I grabbed onto the edge of the tub, fucking him back, grinding my hips down into his.

When his finger eased into my asshole, I gasped, feeling my orgasm only moments away, that gentle probing pushing me closer to the edge. I worked toward it, wanting it, aching for it, my pussy throbbing for release.

"Deeper," I growled, arching my back so he had more of my ass, reaching one hand back to spread it for him. "Shove it in, baby!"

He groaned, pressing his finger further, the water making resistance moot, and I sank my teeth into his shoulder when a second and third finger worked their way in, twisting their way through my flesh.

"Ohhhhh fuck!" I heard myself, almost screaming with it, my whole body taut as our flesh worked together toward that delicious, inevitable end. "Now, baby, ohhhhh yes!"

Sound receded and the wave hit me like a pulse of heat, taking my body over completely, my belly undulating with it, my pussy clenching around his thrusting cock, the tight ring of my asshole working around his fingers until I thought I couldn't stand another moment of it.

"Please," I begged him, pressing against his chest, the sensation so incredible I trembled with it still as I moved away from him, collapsing against the side of the tub and hanging on.

"I think the tub was a good idea," Jack said and I could hear his grin as I pressed my flushed cheek to the cool surface. I couldn't even open my eyes, but I felt his hands on me, running over my shoulders, my back, and I could smell something sweet, like lilacs or lavender.

"What—?" I murmured as his big hands turned me, pulling me to my knees in the tub. His hands were soapy as they ran down my arms and back up, suds spreading over my neck, and down my chest.

"Isn't that the point of a bath?" He smiled, his hands cupping the fullness of my breasts, making me shiver when he thumbed my nipples. "Getting clean?"

"Ohhh yes," I sighed, arching as his soapy hands cupped and kneaded my flesh.

"Stand up," he instructed, and he steadied me as I did, my orgasm and the heat from the tub making me weak. His eyes met mine and I saw something in them I hadn't in years. "My god, you're so beautiful..."

His praise sent more heat through my body, and then he was washing me again, his palms moving over my belly and thighs, between my legs, the gentle sawing motion of his hand there making me tremble.

"Turn around."

I did as he asked, his hands making their way over my lower back, down the soft curve of my ass and hips, spreading my thighs as they made their way toward my knees.

"Bend over." He pressed me forward, and I clung to the edge of the tub, his palms working the smooth cheeks of my behind. "Time to get you really clean..."

"Oh!" I cried as his finger worked its way into my asshole. "Oh, god... honey..."

He didn't stop, pressing another in, working the flesh open with his sudsy fingers. I couldn't resist him or the sensation and my thighs spread wider on their own, my back arching as I moaned and took a third finger into my ass. He kept them there for a while, encouraged by the soft noises I made in my throat, and I groaned when he slowly slid them out again, aching to feel that fullness.

A cascade of water fell over my back and down my bottom, shocking me with its heat, and I looked back to see him pouring it from a cup, rinsing the soap away. His eyes were bright as he watched the water beading over my skin, and I saw his hand moving between his legs and knew he was still so hard. I wanted to reach around and grab him, suck him, devour his cock, but he had other things in mind.

"Jack!" I cried when his tongue found its way between that cleft, working over my wet, puckered asshole.

The heat filling my face didn't have anything to do with the steam rising from the tub, but I couldn't deny how incredible it felt to have his mouth there. I groaned when he made his tongue hard and probed.

"Spread your ass," he said, and I did, ashamed of my own eagerness as I rested my flushed cheek against the cool edge of the tub, using both hands to open myself up for him.

He had complete access now and he took advantage of it, his tongue lapping over the furrowed crease of my asshole and his thumb slipping into my pussy as he rubbed my mound with his fingers. I trembled with the pleasure of it, going up on my tiptoes in an attempt to seek even more sensation.

"Ohhhhh god!" I cried when he started fucking my ass with his tongue, his thumb moving in and out of my pussy with the same easy rhythm. I spread myself even wider, wanting more and getting it, the probing between my cheeks going deeper. I felt the tip of his tongue moving around that tight band of muscle, making me shiver.

"Noooooo," I moaned when he slid his tongue out, but the next sensation jolted me so much I nearly fell over. I probably would have if he hadn't steadied me with his other hand as he pressed something hard and round against the fissured crack of my ass.

"What the hell?" I turned to look and my eyes widened when I saw what he had in his hands. "That wasn't in the toy box!"

"Surprise!" he said with a wink, pressing the first bead on the string further into my ass. They were small beads, probably less than an inch in diameter, but they felt huge as he worked them against the taut opening of my ass.

"Where did those come from?" I gasped, groaning as the pressure began to build as he pressed hard, harder. "What are you—a magician? Did you pull those out of your ass?"

"No," he chuckled. "But they're going into yours..."

"God!" I cried, biting my lip as the first one slipped in. The sensation was strange, different. I felt full there, but not quite completely, so different from his cock or a dildo.

"Ready for another one?" he asked and I shook my head, screwing my eyes shut, but he pressed on anyway, working another bead past that tight ring of muscle. "There..."

I imagined it nestled against the first one inside of me, and then there was another, pushing the rest deeper still as it went, making room, tunneling through. I really felt full now, and something in me wanted them out. I bit my lip, fighting against it and he pressed in yet another.

"Two more," he reassured me as my hands trembled, holding my ass open. I found that if I spread myself wider, he could ease them in better, so I struggled to stay still and relaxed, opening myself up for him.

"Please," I begged, feeling that gentle "pop" as another slid past that taut resistance.

"Almost there, baby," he murmured, kissing my behind as he worked the last one in. I felt his finger go in with it, pressing them deep, and I groaned, squirming.

Panting, I looked back at him, my eyes wide. "Now what?"

"Now...I fuck you senseless." He stood and grabbed my hips. His cock was like steel as he slid into my wetness, my pussy dripping with my juices and his saliva.

The stretch of his cock inside of my pussy made the sensation of the beads buried inside my ass even more pronounced. With every thrust, that feeling of fullness seemed to grow, until I couldn't tell anymore where or how I was being filled, just that I was brimming to capacity, like something swelling and ready to burst.

One of his hands slid under my belly, holding me steady as we rocked. I gripped the edge of the tub, searching for some sort of handhold on the slippery surface. Below us the water churned and sloshed, Jack's weight thrusting into me making even more waves as he fucked me, his low grunting a tell-tale sign that he was getting close.

"Ohhhh god baby!" I moaned when his fingers delved between my pussy lips, searching for and finding my swollen clit. "Yes, fuck me hard!"

I didn't have to ask—he was working my pussy with his cock and his hand now, shoving in deep while he rubbed his finger over and over my aching clit. I had almost forgotten the beads buried inside of my ass when he gave a slight tug on the string, making me squeal and jerk beneath him.

"Hold your ass open for me," he growled, pulling his cock almost all the way out, so the head of him sat pulsing just inside of my pussy.

Whimpering, I wiggled and positioned myself so that both hands were free and I was resting my cheek against the tub again. The tension on the string was incredible—it felt as if he were going to turn me inside out. I used both hands to spread my ass, feeling the tension ease just a little.

"Ohhhhhh fuck," I cried when he slid his cock out and pressed it between my pussy lips, using the head of it to rub at my clit. He knew how much I loved that, the spongy, wet tip making a hot, fleshy trail over that sensitive bud.

He slapped at my cunt with his cock, jerking it roughly a few times against my lips, making me moan, and then found my clit again, rubbing fast and steady. My legs trembled, sensing my impending orgasm, and I panted and writhed and worked toward it, arching my back and rolling my hips. Everything between my legs felt thick and swollen, ready to pop, and then something did—Jack pulled one of the beads out of my ass!

"Ohhhhh GOD!" I moaned, shivering when the thick, round orb slid out of that tight, contracting orifice.

"You like that?" Jack murmured, and then he was kneeling behind me, his face buried up between my legs, his tongue doing the work his cock had been doing just a moment ago, with a much more deft and precise aim.

"Oh baby, you're gonna make me come," I warned him, as if he needed to be cautioned.

He knew just what he was doing, his whole face buried against my pussy, the tension growing as he tugged on the string leading into my ass. The tug grew insistent, a pull and release, and I felt the beads inside of me shifting somehow, as if they were waiting, too.

"Now, oh, now!" I cried, grinding my pussy against his tongue, the sweet pulse of my release beginning to overtake me. He made a deep sound in his throat, still sucking and licking at my flesh, and the tension in my ass became incredible as he pulled—hard—and tugged all of the beads out of my ass in a row.

My orgasm became something else with that motion. What began as a sweet lapping tide coming in became a sudden tidal wave, and I screamed as it hit with the aching sensation of my ass being emptied, each bead popping through that taut ring in quick succession, slipping out of the secret cavern of my ass.

But Jack wasn't done with me. My ass still gaping, my body still shivering with my climax, he stood and slid his cock into the space where the beads had just been. I gasped at the soft insistence of his flesh, so different from the unforgiving demand of the beads, as he tunneled his way past that still pulsing band of muscle, forcing his way deeper into my ass.

"Ohhhh fuck yeah," he groaned, grabbing my hips and sinking deeper still before beginning to move. His hand gripped my wrists and pulled them up behind my back and he held them there while he thrust into me, his cock like a piston driving into my flesh.

"Come inside me," I pleaded, wanting to feel the heat of his cock exploding, filling that hot, aching passage. "Do it, baby, fill my ass with your cum!"

"Oh god," he moaned, his grip tightening as he thrust again, rocking me hard against the edge of the tub, and I felt it, a thick pulse on the underside of his cock as his climax began.

"Yes, yes, yes," I encouraged, squeezing his cock, making him jerk and buck and groan as he emptied himself deep into my belly. He pulled back just a little then, and I felt still more of his cum hitting my ass in hot spurts, leaving a slick trail of heat as it slid down my pussy lips.

With another groan, Jack released me, collapsing down into the tub, and I went with him, crawling into his lap. We rocked in the waves, kissing, still panting, both of us spent.

"We need another bath," I murmured against his ear.

"Hand me the soap," he chuckled, sliding his hands over the rounded swell of my ass.

"I can't," I groaned. "You're going to kill me..."

"But we'll die happy." He smiled, his finger finding and probing me there. I smiled, too, murmuring an agreement and opening for him once again. I just couldn't seem to help myself.

Chapter Six

"Oh my god!" I opened the package and stood staring at the contents, aghast.

We'd seen it today while we were out window shopping, but I never in a million years thought we could afford it. More lingerie than dress, it was something I'd long for but never buy myself, because I just couldn't justify it. Where would I wear it? And if I had somewhere to wear it once, well, did that make it worth the cost? I would spend hours talking myself out of it, all the while longing to try it on, and eventually walk away empty handed.

But Jack had bought it and had it delivered to the hotel. "Red," Jack instructed, holding the panties out to me. "No bra."

I didn't say anything as I took it all into the bathroom, taking off the robe I'd been wearing after our bath and slipping the dress over my head. It was a Valentino with a black silk top, spaghetti straps, but the bottom was sheer lace, form-fitting and long. The red panties would show right through it. *Everything* would show right through it...

I groaned when I pulled the panties on. I'd forgotten they were a thong.

My hair was still slightly damp as I pulled it up and back, twisting it into place and securing it with a beaded wraparound and a long, curved stick. Auburn curls escaped at my temples, framing my face, and I tugged at the top of the dress, worried about the amount of cleavage I was showing with no bra on. Could I really go out dressed like this? Was it even legal?

"Jack?" I pulled open the door tentatively, seeing him shrugging on his dinner jacket. His eyes widened when he saw me, his mouth dropping open.

"Holy hell." He took one step toward me and stopped, transfixed, as I came into the room. I was still barefoot, and the black lace edge of the dress grazed the ground when I wasn't wearing heels. His eyes swept downward and lingered at the red beacon of the panties under the dress. I felt as if I were wearing a neon sign.

"I don't know if I can go out like this." I stepped into a pair of black heels, bending over to buckle the straps. Jack's eyes brightened when I did and I flushed, knowing he could see me, completely exposed except for the thong, from behind. "Where are we going?"

"At the moment, I'm thinking…bed?" He grinned, grabbing me and turning me to him to kiss me. I slipped my arms around his neck, kissing him back, feeling more relaxed in his arms than I had in years.

"So, where are we really going?" I tilted my head so he could access my neck and he gave me shivery kisses down over my collarbone.

"Dinner." He kissed the tops of my breasts. Thankfully the dress had a little built in support, but my nipples were hard and poking into the material. "And I'm having you for dessert."

"No objections from me," I murmured, feeling the crotch of my panties starting to get wet already. I didn't know how I was going to manage to make it through dinner. Jack pocketed his wallet and the key card, opening the door to the hallway and leading me out. We passed an older couple in the corridor carrying luggage toward their room. They didn't appear to notice at first, but then I heard the woman gasp and that turned the man's head. His eyes widened as we passed and she smacked him on the arm, hissing, "Steven!"

"I think that was the dress," I whispered as Jack pushed the elevator button. I saw the man still staring as he fumbled for something in his pockets.

"No." Jack took me by the elbow as we entered the elevator. "It was the woman *in* the dress."

I flushed as the doors whooshed closed, taking us down to the first floor. I thought Jack would lead us to the valet, so they could get our car, but I was surprised when he pulled me past the desk and around the corner. One of the guys working valet raised his eyebrows as we passed, and I blushed, turning my face toward Jack.

"They have a great restaurant here," Jack explained, giving the maître d' our name. I couldn't help but feel everyone's eyes on me and was relieved to see it was relatively empty—only one couple seated in a far corner. Of course, we were early for dinner. Thankfully, it was moderately dark inside, lit only by candles in the center of the tables, and they seated us quite quickly, but I was disappointed there were no booths to hide in, just tables and chairs with open backs.

"I feel so exposed," I whispered. Jack just smiled, perusing his menu. I decided quickly—something small, easy to eat fast, and nothing that would stain—a Chinese chicken salad. When the waiter came by, I was eager to give him my order and get back to our room.

"I'll have—Lloyd." The name escaped my lips in a near whisper and I felt an insidious blush rising from my chest to my cheeks.

The waiter startled, his eyes sweeping over me in surprise and sudden recognition. "Hello again."

I nodded, fanning myself slowly with the menu and hoping I didn't look as red as I felt. "I'll have the Chinese chicken salad…and water. Lots of water."

He nodded, making a note of it, and turned to Jack, who I noticed was grinning from ear to ear. "Porterhouse, medium rare, baked potato, and the lady and I would like a bottle of wine. What would you recommend?"

"The wine menu is here, sir." Lloyd cleared his throat, leaning over and pulling a smaller menu off the table, handing it to Jack. I saw his eyes dip into my cleavage and wondered if he could see the color of my panties through the lace from his angle. I didn't want to look down and draw attention to it to check.

Jack raised his eyebrow. "No recommendations?"

Lloyd looked directly at me, pushing his glasses up. "I'd recommend a red, sir… a red is fuller, it has more body and spirit…" His eyes moved from my hair down to my waist… and lower… and I was sure he could see the color of my panties.

I cleared my throat. "Are you sure you're talking about wine?"

Jack chuckled. "It's true about redheads, too."

"That's what I hear…" Lloyd turned to Jack. "If they're real redheads."

"Oh, I am," I said quickly, used to defending the rich color of my hair.

Lloyd grinned. "Yes, ma'am…I remember."

"Oh…" The memory of standing bent over near the bed with a glass butt plug stuck deep into my ass while he brought in our room service made me dizzy and faint and I fanned myself faster with the menu.

"We'll have a bottle of Dom Perignon." Jack put down the wine menu. I stared at him, blinking fast.

"Will that be all, sir?"

Jack winked. "For now…thanks."

"Oh my god, I'm so embarrassed." I grabbed and covered my face with the wine menu as Lloyd walked away.

"You're beautiful." Jack took the menu from me, putting back on the table. I felt his hand on my knee under the table, rubbing the lace against my bare skin.

"Jack…"

He smiled, his eyes bright. "I want you to do something for me."

"What?" I cocked my head at him, suspicious, and I was right to be.

"Go into the bathroom and take off your panties."

I stared at him. "What?"

"You heard me." He grinned and sat back as Lloyd came to the table with the bottle of wine. He used a corkscrew right there and I jumped when the cork popped, gasping.

"Here you go, ma'am." Lloyd handed a full glass to me as he poured Jack's wine. "Did you know that the very first wine glass was molded from the breast of Helen of Troy?"

"I…" Looking at Jack, I smiled. "I had no idea."

"It's true." Lloyd re-corked the bottle and set it back on ice. "Although later, it's rumored that Marie Antoinette decided to make a new glass molded from her own breast, and the size of the wine glass was considerably increased."

Jack grinned. "Good thing they didn't use yours, honey. We'd have to throw the two-glass rule right out the window."

I flushed. "Jack!"

Lloyd winked at me. "I wouldn't mind drinking from such a lovely, overflowing cup."

I cleared my throat. "Thank you…Lloyd."

When I said his name, he smiled. "You're welcome."

Jack waited until Lloyd had excused himself and was out of earshot to lean in to me and whisper, "Now…go."

"But…Jack…this dress…" I pleaded with my eyes, biting my lip. I had hoped, in the midst of the breast and wine talk, he'd forgotten his request.

"I know." His eyes were full of heat as he looked at me. "I want the whole world to know you're a real redhead."

"Jack!"

"Do it." He insisted, pulling something out of his pocket. It was a small white box, wrapped with a red ribbon around it. "And put this on."

Unable to resist finding out what was in the box, I stood, looking around for the bathroom. It was just a few tables away, through a doorway flanked with two tall, potted rubber tree plants. I slipped through the door marked "Ladies" and stood looking at myself in the full-length mirror for a moment, thinking how far from "ladylike" this dress made me look—or feel. It was incredibly revealing and sexy.

There was no one in the restroom and I pulled the ribbon on the box, opening it, excited. Frowning, I pulled out a little plastic red butterfly with several elastic bands attached, and then saw a note with Jack's handwriting at the bottom of the box. "For you to wear" it said, and had an illustration of just where to put it—and how. I stared at the picture, stunned, sure it couldn't be right, but it had a front and back view, and as technical instructions went, it was pretty darned clear.

I took it into the stall with me, lifting the lace skirt of the dress high up over my hips and slipping the red panties down, stepping out of them. The butterfly centered itself between my legs with a little fleshy nub touching my clit. It had a flexible plastic piece that stretched back with an anal probe attached. I slid that in first, gasping as it entered the tight muscle of my sphincter with no hint of lubrication. It didn't go in far—three or four inches at the most—and it was only as thick as a man's finger. The elastic straps were clear and attached to the butterfly, front and back, to keep it on.

I picked up the panties from the floor and went to the sink to wash my hands. Then I stood in the full length mirror, looking between my legs. The butterfly spread its wings over my pussy lips, leaving the bright red shock of my pubic hair showing above it. You could definitely see I was a real redhead all right, even through the black lace. The thought of going back out into the restaurant like this was both exciting and almost too humiliating to imagine.

I gasped when I opened the door, finding Lloyd standing outside of it. "I'm sorry!"

"Your husband…" Lloyd looked down between my legs, his eyes drawn there like a magnet. The red panties were gone, but my pubic hair showed through the lace, as did the little butterfly wings. "Asked me…to check…"

"I'm fine." I balled the red panties up tighter in my hand. "Thank you."

He nodded, stepping back and letting me pass.

"Perfect." Jack smiled when I walked back to the table, sitting carefully as the probe pushed deeper into my ass, the butterfly kissing my clit. "Like it?"

"It's...different." I took a gulp of wine, glancing around the table and then tossing the panties across the table to him. "Did you...did you send that waiter...?"

He smiled, slipping them into his jacket pocket. "I just wanted to make sure you were okay."

I raised my eyebrows at him. "I wasn't gone that long."

"Chinese chicken salad." Lloyd set the plate in front of me, and another in front of Jack. "Porterhouse...is there anything else I can get for you?"

I shook my head, picking up my fork and starting to eat. Jack was clearly enjoying himself, but I wanted to finish and get back to the room as quickly as we could. Playing sex games in the hotel room was one thing, but playing sex games in public? I was afraid we'd get kicked out—or arrested. The thought of trying to explain to my parents, who were watching the kids, why they had to bail Jack and I out of jail, was just too humiliating to contemplate.

"That will be all, thanks." Jack gave him a nod, picking up his wine glass. "If you need anything, just ask for—"

I gasped out loud and nearly came off my seat when the butterfly between my legs began to vibrate. Both men looked at me, Lloyd's eyes wide with surprise, Jack's glinting mischievously.

"Are you all right?" Lloyd asked.

"Just...spicy..." I nodded, eyes widening as the vibration increased, and the soft buzz between my legs became clearly audible. I looked at Jack, panicked, but he just sat back and grinned, one hand still on his wine glass, the other in his coat pocket.

Lloyd looked doubtfully at my Chinese chicken salad—which wasn't spicy in the least. "Do you want me to take it back for you?"

"No, no." I shook my head, desperate to get rid of him, waving him away. "It's fine, really—it just...surprised me."

He nodded, still looking puzzled, his eyes dipping downward as I wiggled in my chair. I knew he could hear it—he *had* to be able to hear it. I felt it buzzing noisily against my clit, the soft nub rubbing back and forth when I moved. Lloyd's eyes drifted slowly upwards, meeting mine, and I swallowed when I saw the dawning realization on his face.

"Well, if there's anything you need from me," he said with a small smile. "You just let me know."

"Will do." Jack grinned and winked at me, but I looked down at my plate, unable to ignore the feeling between my thighs anymore. My clit responded to the growing hum, my nipples hardening against the silk fabric of the dress.

"Thanks," I whispered, leaning my hand against my forehead and looking desperately at Jack. Lloyd walked slowly away, glancing over his shoulder at us, and I waited until he'd gone into the kitchen before speaking.

"Turn it off!" I hissed as I watched Jack cut into his steak. Every time I shifted in my seat, the butterfly kissed my clit, sending shivers through me.

"Are you sure?" He lifted his fork to his mouth, eyes on mine as he chewed. I bit my lip, glancing around as I moved my hips, back and forth, forcing that fleshy nub to rub against my clit. God, it felt good...

"Not here, Jack," I pleaded, in spite of the delightful sensation between my legs. It was just too humiliating to bear.

"Okay." He sighed, reaching into his pocket. Relieved, I held my breath, waiting for the buzzing to stop.

"Jack!" I nearly screamed his name, sitting up straight, eyes wide, when the probe in my ass began to rotate. Lloyd peeked his head out of the kitchen, blinking at us, and I bit my lip to keep from crying out.

"Did you need something?" Lloyd came over to the table and I groaned softly as the probe found some deep, secret place in me, pressing there again and again.

"No, no." I waved him away. The aching buzz between my legs was hard enough to ignore, but the insistent turning of the probe in my ass was impossible not to respond to. "Please…please go away… god… okay?" I pleaded, closing my eyes and squirming in my chair.

"Feel good, baby?" Jack whispered, and I knew Lloyd must be gone, but I didn't want to open my eyes to see.

"Yes," I whispered back, leaning my forehead on my palm again, thinking I could hide my pleasure somehow. It was too good to ignore and my hips began to rock all on their own, forcing the butterfly to kiss my clit and the probe deeper into my ass.

"That's it," Jack urged, and the probe began to rotate faster, making me moan softly and shake my head, trying to deny it. "God, you're beautiful."

"Ohh no," I breathed, arching my back and grazing my hard nipples against the edge of the table. I didn't want to do this, to come here in the middle of the restaurant, but there was nothing I could do. My body wasn't under my own control and my response was involuntary, my thighs beginning to quiver, my breath coming faster.

"He's watching you," Jack murmured and my eyes flew open. He jerked his head toward the bathrooms and I turned my head slowly, at first not seeing anything through the haze of my own pleasure. Then I glimpsed Lloyd's dark head through the leaves of one of the rubber tree plants. My eyes dropped slowly, drawn by a motion behind the trunk. For a moment, I was too distracted by the steady pulse between my thighs and wasn't sure what I was seeing. A hot wave went through me when I realized Lloyd's hand was cupping his crotch through his dark waiter's pants, rubbing himself there.

"Oh god," I whispered as the buzzing grew between my legs, the probe sinking deeper into my ass as I shifted my hips in the chair. Jack took his hand out of his jacket pocket and cut himself another piece of steak as he watched me. I looked up at him. "Please…"

"My cock is so hard right now." He said it casually, taking another sip of wine, but the thought made me groan out loud. Watching me giving into the rising sensation between my legs was arousing him, and that just served to intensify my pleasure. "I bet Lloyd's is, too…"

I glanced over toward the bathrooms, surprised to see Lloyd sliding the zipper down on his slacks. He was only partially hidden by the plant, and if anyone walked in or out of the bathroom, they would be sure to see him. I looked around the restaurant with half-closed eyes. The couple in the corner was in the middle of their dinner and hadn't seemed to notice anything. The maître d' was out in the alcove near the front of the restaurant—I couldn't see him at all. Apparently, we were alone, at least for the moment.

But that was the last time I was going to be able to assess whether or not it was safe to do what we were doing—because when I glanced over and saw Lloyd's hand moving up and down the considerable length of his exposed cock, I lost any more ability to think or reason or stop what was happening. Instead, I rested my head on my arms on the table, moaning softly as the butterfly buzzed hungrily against my clit, hoping I looked like I was just resting or was perhaps feeling a bit ill.

What I was feeling, however, was the opposite. I couldn't control how fast my breath was coming or the soft, whimpering noises my throat insisted on making as my body climbed higher and higher toward climax. I glanced at Lloyd stroking himself, faster and faster as he watched me rocking as subtly as I could against my chair. I was starting to lose all sense of where I was, my pussy on fire, my ass clenching in response to the rotating probe.

"Jack," I whimpered, sitting up and grabbing onto the edges of my chair. "Oh honey, I—"

I heard Jack's breath, too, coming fast as he watched me, his eyes full of lust. I swear I heard Lloyd breathing heavy, too, just a few tables away, jerking himself off behind the rubber tree plant. I arched my back, biting my lip to keep from crying out as I came, shuddering on my chair as the relentless buzzing between my legs went on and on. My pussy clamped down in sweet, continuous waves, making my ass clench and pull the probe even deeper.

"Ohhh baby, my ass," I moaned out loud, rocking faster, unable to stop. Jack's eyes widened as I gripped the edge of the table, fucking against the sweet, turning probe in my ass that was making me shudder uncontrollably. "Ohhh Jack, I'm gonna come in my ass!"

I was apparently loud enough to make the couple in the back corner look around, but I didn't notice then— Jack told me about it later. I was too focused on riding it out, shoving my bottom down in the chair, wanting more, deeper, harder, god, I couldn't stand it, I was so close, almost there, and suddenly I was bucking and arching as I came, completely lost, giving myself over as my body shuddered in the chair. I moaned, I heard myself moaning and couldn't stop it, grabbing the edge of the table so hard it shook in my hands.

"Oh my god," I heard Jack whisper. I opened my eyes, my whole body flushed with heat and I watched, breathless, as Lloyd stiffened and came, too, his cock spraying the trunk of the rubber tree plant with the first blast. I gasped out loud, still quivering with my own climax, watching with rapt attention as the next few waves spurted hotly into the soil of the pot below.

"Jack, turn it off!" I hissed, glaring at him, flushed, still panting, but he just grinned. "You! God!" I stood, feeling so dizzy I had to grip the table to keep from falling. The butterfly continued to hum until I reached the ladies room door, pushing past Lloyd, who was still zipping himself up and straightening, looking very red in the face.

Then, finally, it stopped. I stood in front of the mirror, leaning against the bathroom sink, looking at my flushed cheeks, my breasts rising and falling fast under black lace, still stunned by what had just happened. Who was this woman in the mirror, the one who had always done the right things, who was nothing but an ordinary wife and mother and elementary school teacher trying to build a life with her husband in the normal, suburban world? Did I even know her?

My eyes were wild, still full of lust, and I felt it. The tiny clitoral vibrator between my legs began to buzz, ever so gently. It was so soft I couldn't even hear it, but I felt it, and knew it was Jack, calling me. My pussy hummed in response. I was soaking wet, my thighs sticky with my juices, and god help me, I wanted more. Whatever place I had discovered inside myself over the past few months, a place I couldn't have imagined in the deepest, darkest recesses of my imagination, had become home.

I tucked a few auburn curls into place before taking a deep breath and heading out of the bathroom again. When I got back to the table, at least a little more composed, although unable to keep the humiliating blush from my cheeks, Jack had our food wrapped and ready to go.

"Come on." He held out his hand to me and grabbed the bottle of wine off the table. "Let's go do dessert."

I groaned softly as he led me out and I saw Lloyd when I glanced furtively back over my shoulder, standing in the alcove with the maître d', his dark eyes hungry as he watched us depart.

Chapter Seven

He kissed me in the elevator, pressing his hard cock against my crotch, grinding that fluttering butterfly against my pussy. We were alone—thank god, because I don't think he would've stopped, even if we hadn't been, and I didn't want him to. There was a mirror against the back wall, and I watched us over his shoulder as we rocked together, a couple locked in a lustful embrace, almost as if I were standing outside of myself.

"Jack!" I gasped when he reached over and pushed the emergency stop button, the alarm sounding. "What—?"

But he didn't give me time to answer. Turning me around, he shoved me up against the mirror, yanking my expensive dress up over the bare expanse of my ass, and kneeling down to bury his face against my pussy. Oh god! The vibrator between my legs, barely buzzing before, began to hum louder as Jack shoved his face into my pussy, fucking me with his tongue, his nose pressing the rotating probed deeper into my aching ass.

"Oh god!" I spread wider for him, hanging onto the railing across the back of the elevator, looking at myself through half closed eyes. Who was this women exposing herself in a public elevator and letting her husband lick her…oh…god…*fuck* her…

Jack stood, the food and wine on the floor beside us as he unzipped and shoved his cock into my cunt, impaling me, pulling my hips back to meet his. I moaned, arching to take him, the buzz against my clit driving me crazy, taking me closer and closer to yet another orgasm.

"What a pretty little fuckslut you are," he murmured, his gaze moving over my image in the mirror, my breasts swaying as he slammed into me, my cheek pressed to the mirror, my heated, panting breath fogging the surface. "You like being my fuckslut, don't you?" I groaned, closing my eyes, knowing he was right and feeling humiliated at the thought. But I did like it—more than that, I loved it.

"Tell me." I felt his hands gripping my breasts as he fucked me, faster, harder, driving the rotating probe deep into my ass, the persistent hum against my clit making me writhe with pleasure. "Tell me, you little whore!"

I groaned, flushing, spreading wider and working my ass back against him, grinding, feeling myself letting go completely, not caring where we were, who I thought I was or wanted everyone to think I was. There was nothing but me and Jack and the sweet, rising sensation building between us. In that moment, in every moment, I was completely his.

"Yes!" I nearly screamed the word, his hand in my hair, pulling my head back so he could turn my face to his and kiss me, hard, bruising, his cock swelling inside of me. I gasped, meeting his lust filled eyes with mine. "Yes, I love being your little fuckslut. I'm your little whore, Jack. I'm your nasty, dirty little girl. Fuck me good and hard, baby. Make me come all over your cock!"

He groaned at the words, his tongue plunging almost as deep into my mouth as his cock was buried in my pussy, and I came then, my screams of pleasure muffled as Jack spent himself inside of me, his shuddering weight pressing us both forward against the mirror, his cock throbbing deep in me.

"Oh fuck." He panted as he tucked and zipped, releasing the emergency stop.

I didn't move, hanging onto the railing, feeling my dress sliding back down over my behind, and Jack's cum slowly moving downward, too. I stood there, trying to catch my breath, until the bell sounded for our floor and the doors opened. Jack moved to put an arm around me, guiding me out and down the hall to our room. He had, thankfully, turned the vibrator off, and the butterfly was quiet against my swollen clit as Jack juggled everything to put the keycard in the door and opened it.

I went immediately to the bed, collapsing there, belly first. I heard Jack chuckle as he put our leftover food in the little fridge and stowed the wine, but I didn't move. Just remembering what had happened made me flush again with lust—my god, what were we doing here, my husband and I? What exactly were we doing?

"Ready for bed?" He lay beside me, on his back, loosening his tie, smiling up at the ceiling. I turned my head, resting my cheek against my arm, so full of him, still, I could barely breathe. And still, I wanted more. I loved my husband, I had loved him since the moment I saw him, I think, sitting across from me in a very boring college Lit class, but I couldn't remember feeling this way before, so full and empty of him all at once.

"Bed..." I murmured. "Bathtubs...restaurants...elevators...it doesn't matter to me..."

He turned toward me, up on his elbow, his hand moving over the lacy material of my dress, down my back, over the swell of my behind. His gaze followed, and I saw the hunger there, the same ache I was feeling, I think. We'd sparked something between us that had moved from a slow burn toward something more like a wild fire, out of control.

"More?" His fingers dragged my dress up over my thighs, my ass, exposing me, and I sighed happily.

"Always."

The toy was quiet now, but out of the corner of my eye, I saw Jack reach into his pocket and so I knew what was coming as it jumped to life again. I shivered, my hips already moving in response.

"Such a hungry slut," he murmured, turning me over on the bed. I let him, willing to do anything now, lost in desire and sensation. He put my feet up on the bed—I was still wearing the strappy black heels—spreading my thighs into a wide butterfly, mimicking the toy between my legs. I groaned softly when the anal probe began to turn, touching deep, soft places in me, bringing them alive.

"God I love your cunt." Jack knelt beside the bed, and I felt his hot breath, such a sweet anticipation. "Do you like your new toy?"

"*My* new toy?" I laughed softly, going up on my elbows so I could look down at him. "You're sure having a lot of fun playing with it, even if you claim it's mine."

"Can't deny that," he agreed, reaching into his pocket again, making me arch and gasp by turning it up. "Your pleasure is my single greatest joy, sweetheart."

"Ohhh god!" My head went back, my eyes closing, gasping, "That works out well, then, doesn't it?"

"I'll say." His fingers slid into my wetness—and I was wet. Beyond wet, really. My dress was pulled up to my waist, my panties gone, still in Jack's pocket presumably, and I was completely exposed to him, trembling with a longing I couldn't even begin to articulate. His hand moved, fingers in and out, first two, then three, mimicking the motion of fucking, making me rock with him.

"Can you take another?" he asked, twisting his hand, pressing his fingers together and sliding them—all four of them—deep inside, stretching me wide.

"Ahhhhh god!" I gasped at the sensation, so very open, my flesh becoming more elastic as he worked his fingers into my pussy. "Jack! Oh! It's too much!"

"Where have I heard that before?" he mused, and I heard the click of a K-Y tube being opened and glanced down in a panic. He was applying it liberally to my pussy and his hand as he slipped deeper—all four of his fingers moving slowly in and out—stretching me to the breaking point.

"What are you doing?" I gasped as he tossed the tube aside, his eyes bright as he twisted his hand, pressing, forcing me to spread wider. "Ohhh! Jack!"

"Just relax," he murmured, moving to one knee on the bed, his hand still buried inside me, up to his knuckles now, his thumb tucked under as he pushed hard, forcing my flesh to yawn open in response. There was pain with every inch of ground he gained, an uncomfortable feeling of fullness, but the competitive pleasure of the fluttering butterfly against my clit helped combat it.

"Please," I whimpered, back on my elbows, watching as my husband's hand seemed to disappear between my legs. "Oh god, please..."

"Let me..." His eyes met mine, and I bit my lip, remembering the first time he put his cock fully into my ass, how much trust it took, how much effort. "Let me in..."

"Ohhhh yes," I whispered, focused on relaxing everything between my legs, opening to him completely, not fighting anymore, and I was amazed how easy it was for him to slide his fist all the way inside. His knuckles were nubs moving deep as he twisted his hand, back and forth, watching my face.

"Like that?"

I groaned, nodding, unable to speak. The sensation was too much, so intense I thought I might die as he started to move his hand in and out in of my pussy, beginning to fuck me, this time not with his fingers, or his cock, but with his *entire fist*. He was slow at first, just like he'd been the first time he put his cock in my ass, but that didn't last long.

Because I liked it. More than that, I wanted it, and I couldn't hide my body's response. I began to fuck him back, rocking my hips on the bed against his hand, driving him deeper into my pussy. I'd never felt so full, but I wanted more and more of him, thrusting into me, taking me, giving me the most intense pleasure I'd ever experienced.

"Ohhh Jack it's soooo good!" I moaned, collapsing completely back on the bed, arms thrown over my head, pushing my hips way up to meet his driving, twisting fist. My ass was completely off the bed, rolling, rocking, grinding him faster, and just when I thought it couldn't get any better, the buzz between my legs grew impossibly loud, jolting my clit alive, taking me to the edge of bliss.

"Ooooooooooooooooooooo!" I howled, I couldn't help it, feeling it coming, thinking I might explode with the anticipation as my orgasm hovered somewhere unsprung in my lower belly.

"Come on, baby," he encouraged, his breath coming almost as fast as mine. "Do it! I want to feel you come."

"I can't..." I really thought it was impossible, that my climax would stick somewhere behind his fist, because I was so full, stretched so impossibly wide, to my very limit, but it did come, deep and hard and in enormous tidal waves, my pussy contracting around his fist, drawing it in deeper. I thrashed on the bed, thrusting up to meet him, my pussy on fire, even my asshole spasming around the probe still pressed up into it.

It went on and on. And I never wanted it to end. Finally, Jack turned down the volume on the toy, making me whimper and twist. His hand slowly uncurled in me, unfurled, really, sliding easily out, much more easily than it had gone in. The absence of him made me ache, both inside and out.

"That..." Jack moved in beside me to kiss me, pushing up my dress to rest his soaking wet hand against my lower belly, still fluttering with my orgasm. "Was the most beautiful fucking thing I've ever seen in my life."

I smiled, eyes still closed. "Felt pretty good, too."

He unstrapped the toy, and I groaned when the butterfly no longer kissed my clit and the probe slid out of my trembling asshole.

"Wonder if I could do that..." I heard him drop it to the floor, but his finger stayed there, gently teasing the round, flexing hold of my ass. "Here..."

I groaned, my eyes fluttering open, shivering at the thought. My pussy could accommodate him – fingers, cock, even his whole damn hand. It was made to do that, to stretch wide, to take him in. But my ass? I couldn't even begin to imagine...

But something in me didn't balk or recoil. Something in me was saying, vehemently, unequivocally, "Yes!"

"Anything you want." I wrapped an arm around his neck, kissing him, breathing in his familiar scent, his finger still teasing, probing, and even if I'd wanted to, I found I couldn't close myself up the way I once used to anymore.

* * * *

I was luxuriating in the enormous Jacuzzi tub when our breakfast came to the door. The room service I'd expected, but I was surprised to see Lloyd wheel it in. Jack made small talk with him at the door, but I saw Lloyd glancing over at me. He couldn't see anything— certainly far less than he'd seen when he walked into our room last time, and nothing compared to the scene in the dining room the night before! Still, there was a look in his eyes I recognized, and it made me flush with both pleasure and embarrassment.

"Enjoy your breakfast, Mrs. Johnson," he called from the doorway, giving me a wink and a wave.

"Call me Charlie." I smiled, seeing the way his eyes dipped toward the water, where the bubbles I'd poured in covered the surface, although my breasts floated gently, the suds just covering my nipples. "What are you doing working again? Double shift?"

He rolled his eyes and shrugged. "New kid called in sick, so I came in."

"Awww." I tsked appropriately, seeing Jack watching me too, his eyes widening when I stood in the tub, water and suds sheeting down my body. Both men were transfixed, and my body felt the heat of their gaze. "You know what they say about all work and no play..."

I took my time reaching for the towel—nice, for a hotel, thick and luxurious—turning to do so, making sure they both saw a good view from behind as I did. I thought I heard Lloyd groan softly before I wrapped it around me and turned back toward them both.

"I'm here a lot," Lloyd admitted, watching me step out of the tub. "Gotta pay for school."

I padded toward them, meeting Jack's eyes for a moment. He looked both amused and annoyed by my display, and it made me want to laugh. Two could play his game, I thought with a smile, lifting one of the silver lids on the tray.

"What are you going to school for?" The towel slipped down a little over my breasts, almost exposing my nipples, and I didn't correct it as I plucked a strawberry off the fruit platter, enjoying the way the young man in the doorway shifted uneasily from foot to foot at my indiscretion.

"Engineering," Lloyd managed, his eyes glued to the strawberry making its way to my waiting mouth. I sucked on the tip for a moment, licking it, teasing him with both my tongue and my eyes before biting into the juicy fruit.

"Mmmm!" I licked strawberry juice from the corner of my mouth. "There's nothing sexier than a smart man."

He blushed, then, and I had to hide a smile, finishing my strawberry. "Uh...thanks."

"Yeah, thanks, Lloyd," Jack said, stepping between us and guiding Lloyd toward the exit. I turned from them both, still smiling and not hiding it anymore, dropping the towel as I walked toward the bed. I heard Lloyd respond—a small sigh, or intake of breath. It was hard to tell. But I knew he'd seen, and that was enough.

"You're a very bad girl," Jack scolded after he'd tipped the waiter and shut the door, coming to join me on the bed. "Teasing him that way. Poor guy's going to have blue balls all day."

"That's a shame," I agreed, sitting cross-legged on the bed and reaching up to let my hair down—I'd put it up for the bath.

Jack sat across from me, his eyes moving up my body to meet mine. I saw him studying me, wondering. "You'd do it, wouldn't you, if I asked?"

"Do what?"

"Let him fuck you in front of me."

I startled, putting my hair clip down on the night stand. "I…"

Would I? The fantasy was hot, I had to admit. The thought of two men, two cocks, four hands and two sets of lusting eyes…that thought set my pussy on fire. But the reality? I wasn't so sure.

"Would you be okay with that?" I asked, really curious. "Wouldn't you get…jealous?"

Jack shrugged, his eyes dipping down again, following the swell of my breasts, the curve of my belly. "I don't think so. I mean…you're mine. I know that. You know that."

My whole body felt like it was smiling at his words.

"I think it would be hot to share you with another man."

I smiled, leaning back onto the plethora of pillows. "Now who's being bad?"

He grabbed my ankle in one hand, then the other, spreading my legs. "Oh, I get much, much badder."

"That's grammatically incorrect." I groaned when he started kissing up my shin, over my knee. "It's 'more bad.'"

"Way more bad," he agreed, starting to make circles over my thigh with his tongue.

I sighed happily when his tongue parted the red hair between my legs, probing into my wetness. "We're not going anywhere today, either, are we?"

"Nuh-uh." His tongue flattened against my clit, moving slowly back and forth, making me shiver. "I've got a surprise for you."

"I don't think I can take another one."

His head came up, and he was grinning again, his eyes lit up. "I think you'll like it."

I laughed as he hopped off the bed, heading toward the closet. "I've liked them all," I admitted, watching him take bags out. "I just don't know if I'm going to survive the weekend."

"Oh you'll live," he assured me, bringing a flat case over to the bed, unzipping it. Puzzled, I watching him plug in and turn on his laptop, leaving it on the bed. "You'll just be…a little sore."

"What is that?" I watched him set something up on the television on top of the dresser. "Is that…?"

"A web cam."

When I turned toward the laptop again, I saw myself, stretched out on the hotel bed, the laptop sitting beside me.

"Wireless," he explained, hitting a few buttons on the computer, opening another window. "I thought you might like to give the world a little show."

I stared at him, aghast. "Are you insane?"

"Well, you sure liked it when Lloyd was watching you." He shrugged, typing something into the keyboard, and I rolled over onto my belly to watch what he was doing, stunned to find the screen full of smaller windows, each showing a couple in various states of undress, or…worse.

"What is this?" I whispered, fascinated in spite of myself, feeling my pussy clench as I watched a woman sucking her man's cock in one of the smaller windows.

"Which one?" Jack asked, moving the cursor around. "You pick."

"Are these videos?" I pointed to the cocksucking one. She was really going at it, taking almost all of him into her mouth.

"Nope." Jack clicked, and the screen opened up wide, like a television, and with another click, we could hear sound. "It's live."

"Live?" I stared, incredulous, as the couple moved toward the bed in the background. The camera stayed static, showing the man sitting on the edge of the bed, the woman kneeling between his legs, continuing to work on his cock. I heard him groan, the sound of her sucking him filling the speakers.

"Can they hear us?" I whispered.

"No." Jack smiled. "Not yet."

Turning my head, I stared at him. "What's that supposed to mean?"

"Well, if you wanted to…I could open one of these rooms, these windows. And people could watch us."

I shook my head, denying the possibility, but watched, fascinated, glancing at the bottom of the screen, where a fast-moving stream of words flipped by. "What's that?"

"Chat," Jack explained. "People talking to them. Encouraging them. Telling them what they want to see."

"Can they—?"

But on screen, I saw the man leaning over, typing something on the laptop on the night stand. His words appeared in a different color—green instead of white—on the line below. "Want to see me fuck her?"

The typed chorus of *"YES!"* and *"Fuck yeah!"* and *"Do that bitch!"* on the screen was, in fact, nearly unanimous, except for one lone holdout, who typed, *"Lick her first!"*

"Oh my god," I whispered, watching him pull her up onto the bed, bend her over, so she was perpendicular to the camera, her breasts pointing to the bed below her. She was a pretty woman—long dark hair, small breasts, thin. "I can't believe they're doing this!"

"Isn't it hot?" Jack slid a hand down my back to squeeze my ass. "God, I'd love to show you off like that."

"You would?" I flushed, my ass clenching involuntarily under his touch. "Oh but Jack...what if someone recognized us?"

Being an elementary school teacher had its limits, I realized, in this realm.

"They wouldn't have to see your face," he said, moving his fingers slowly between my ass cheeks, making me spread my legs. "Just your sweet little ass from behind."

I licked my lips, contemplating, seeing the words flashing by at the bottom of the screen. *"Fuck her hard!"* and *"Oh damn, that makes my cock so hard,"* and *"I wish I had some of that right now."* There were men out there watching, maybe alone, maybe with their wives or girlfriends, like we were right now. Watching and getting turned on, probably masturbating. The thought was intoxicating. Would men watch me and say the same things?

"Come on, baby." Jack's finger pressed the rim of my asshole, making me shiver. "Let's give them a great show."

I groaned as the tip of his finger slipped into my ass, relenting, lifting my hips. "Okay."

He typed something on the screen with one hand, and suddenly there we were, stretched out on our bellies, Jack's hand moving between my ass cheeks, me completely nude, Jack in a pair of black boxers, the laptop open in front of us on the bed.

"Get up on your hands and knees."

I did as he instructed, seeing my ass fill the screen as I drew closer to the web cam positioned behind us. My pussy glistened in the light—I was wet. I couldn't deny my excitement if I tried.

"Here, you can talk to them..." Jack positioned the laptop in front of me. "While you can still type, anyway..."

"Can they hear us?"

Jack's hand moved over my ass. I felt it, and could watch it on the screen at the same time. "Do you want me to turn on the mic, then?"

There were people joining the "chat" at the bottom of the screen. *"Nice ass!"* one said. *"Hot little pussy!"* said another.

"Yeah," I breathed, pulling a pillow over so I could rest my cheek on it, my ass high in the air. This way I could watch the words on the screen, and I was sure no one could see my face.

Jack did something on the laptop, and then his hand was back between my legs again, rubbing my asshole, round and round. I moaned softly, arching, watching him do it onscreen, never privy to this view before. It was beyond sexy.

"Tell us how much you like it!" someone typed.

"Oh yeah, finger my ass," I moaned, watching Jack spread my pussy juices upward to my asshole. "You know I love it!"

"Yesssss!" appeared on the screen. *"Can you take more than a finger up there?"*

I snorted a laugh, reaching back and spreading myself with both hands. "Show him, baby."

I heard the distinct "pop" of a K-Y tube being opened, but I didn't look back. I could see everything he was doing right there on the screen. The lube slid down the crack of my ass in a fat, wet glop. Jack rubbed it in, first with his finger, and then with the clear, glass butt plug, making me shiver with its cool, slick insistence.

I winced at my own resistance—still, still!—as Jack worked the toy around, easing the opening wider with every pass.

"Ohhhh wait," I groaned as he stretched me fully to the plug's greatest width—I knew, not just from the feeling, but from seeing it on the screen, my asshole gaping around the glass. It was one last push, and it would be inside, but I needed to concentrate on relaxing.

On the screen, words flashed by: *put it in!* and *open up, baby!* And *oh my fucking god her ass is so hot!* I moaned through stretch and burn, arching my back, pressing against Jack's hand and feeling the last bit slip past the tight ring of muscle. The plug filled my ass completely, and I writhed on the bed with the sensation, my pussy on fire, aching to be touched.

Jack seemed to know, because I heard a familiar buzz, and then the rabbit vibrator was sliding into me. I watched it on the screen, opening the pink flesh of my pussy wide—oh my god, the feeling of fullness was almost too much to bear! I whimpered as the rabbit ears touched my clit, humming there as Jack began to fuck me in short, fast strokes.

"You like those two holes filled?" he asked, his voice thick. He was off camera, so I couldn't see him, but I heard his hand moving on his cock, and knew how much this was turning him on. And not just him—the "chat room" was filling up with people, all sitting in their living rooms or bedrooms, watching me get fucked with a dildo on their computer screens. I imagined them—twenty men, thirty?—doing just what Jack was doing, hands shuttling up and down hard, aching lengths of flesh.

My pussy throbbed at the thought and I ground my hips, fucking him back harder.

"Oooooh, god, I'm so close!" I gasped, working my pussy against the vibrator, everything stretched so wide, my breath coming faster. "Make me come! Please! Oh!"

Jack turned the vibrator up full blast, sending me immediately over the edge. I bucked out my orgasm on the bed, watching my ass moving on the screen through half-closed eyes, the pleasure so intense I could barely see at all, and it only increased when Jack grabbed the butt plug and yanked, making me scream with surprise and sensation, leaving my asshole gaping, flexing, twitching for the camera as I came.

The men on the screen were going crazy with lust—their words flashed before me, making me flush. *Holy fuck! Look at that gaper!* and *Jesus Christ I want to fuck that!* and *oh shit I'm gonna cum!* Then Jack was fucking me, not giving me any time to move or breathe or think, the vibrator still shoved deep in my pussy, buzzing relentlessly, and my husband jammed his cock deep into my wide-open asshole.

For a moment, I saw just Jack's ass filling the screen, but then he positioned himself a little above me, standing on the bed, his feet pressed against my knees, fucking my ass at a deep, downward angle.

"Oh god!" I gasped, loving the hot, fleshy feel of his cock compared to the unforgiving length of the dildo. He grunted with every thrust, and I glanced back, seeing his eyes on the screen—he was watching himself fuck me.

"God you're so good and tight," he moaned, slowing a little, and I whimpered, wanting more, reaching between my legs so I could grab the vibrator and fuck myself with it. Being filled and fucked by two hard cocks was incredible, and for a moment I imagined Lloyd beneath me, thrusting himself up into my pussy while Jack fucked my ass, and the thought spurred me on toward yet another orgasm, my pussy clenching the dildo.

The screen was flashing so fast I could barely see what the men there were typing, but excitement was high, and I saw a lot of *"gonna cummmm!"* and *"cum all over her ass!"* I ground my hips back, making him fuck me harder, deeper, and begged him for it.

"Do it!" I pleaded, gasping for air, not caring. "Ohhh fuck me hard! Deep! Take that ass!"

Jack growled at my words, making me take him all the way to the hilt, and still, I wanted more. The vibrator in my pussy was at maximum force, and I fucked myself furiously with it, my nipples rubbing against the comforter on the bed with the motion, sending delicious sparks down between my legs. I was so close. So very close.

"Ohhhh fuck, baby, I'm gonna come!" Jack warned.

I grunted, moving my hips down toward the bed, sliding him out of me. "Come on my ass!"

He slid all the way out with a sweet, sucking sound, his cum already spilling from the end of his cock. I felt it, hot and sticky against my asshole, and I saw it, too, on the computer screen, the tip of his cock bursting open with every wave, raining a white hot shower of cum over the gaping hole of my ass. The deluge of his cum spread downward over my pussy, around the pink stretch where the vibrator was still shoved deep. His cum was still hot when it reached my aching clit, where I pressed the little buzzing rabbit ears with deep concentration.

"Oh!" I nearly jumped out of my own skin in surprise when I felt Jack's tongue in my asshole, lapping at his cum, and that sent me flying, my orgasm closing my eyes against all the hot, dirty words on the screen: *fuck yeah! God she's such a good, nasty little whore! I'm gonna cum alloverherfuckingasssssss!* It was all too good, and I let myself go, pure sensation, my body rocking and rolling and twisting all on its own in a flood of ecstasy.

I don't remember much after that for a while. I know Jack turned the camera off and washed and put the toys and computer away. I panted on the bed, catching my breath, still feeling as if I was flying, until he wheeled the tray over.

"Breakfast?"

"Breakfast?" I sighed happily, looking over at him sitting on the edge of the bed. "My god, I can't believe it isn't lunch time yet."

He chuckled, leaning over and kissing the rounded swell of my behind. "Oh, no, baby...we've got a lot to do before then. I've got a couple more surprises for you."

More!

I groaned, but I was smiling. I couldn't help it. I was going to die in a hotel room in Cleveland, I decided, a deliriously satisfied but seriously dehydrated woman, probably found with her behind still up in the air as an offering to her insatiable husband—and I didn't even care. Our sex life had suddenly become too tempting to resist.

Chapter Eight

I was in love with Jack all over again. I think we were looking at each other with new eyes for the first time in years—endless revolutions of routine, work and kids—and I almost felt like we were on a second honeymoon that weekend. Or really, perhaps, our first, since the time after our wedding was spent studying and taking exams, although we'd had our fair share of intimate breaks in between.

Jack couldn't seem to take his eyes off me. The attention was intoxicating, and I felt myself moving differently, more deliberately, a slow, constant, seductive tease. For years I'd been throwing my hair up into the mommy-ponytail, wearing jeans and sweatshirts around the house and practical cotton panties underneath. I'd moved easily from the good, polite college co-ed, into the role of stable, dependable elementary school teacher, as well as Jack's wife and the mother of his children, without thinking much about it.

But I was thinking about it now.

The woman in the mirror staring back at me, the one whose cleavage nearly spilled out of the red satin dress her husband had purchased earlier that day, the one whose thigh was exposed when she walked because the slit in that same dress was just shy of indecently high, who turned heads like she hadn't in years when she walked down the hotel hallway—even when she *wasn't* dressed to the nines—that woman was me.

I'd forgotten all about her. In fact, I'd pretty much buried her under lists of things to do and papers to grade and meals to make. I'd forgotten what it was like to be attractive, to *feel* attractive. That last was more than half the equation, I decided, rubbing a fine gloss over the plump swell of my lips with a fingertip. The accoutrements were secondary. It was feeling the heat in your body that counted. When I walked, it felt as if the world hung on the swing of my hips, my whole body a beacon of light, drawing moths to the flame.

My husband was drunk with it. Hell, so was I. And so, I found, was our young waiter friend, who we'd mercilessly teased to the breaking point. I could see it in their eyes—both men were positively wolfish, fighting to hold out my chair at dinner, a brief struggle for control, and the incident would stay with me, come to me later, remind me how men fight over women, how much they lust and are willing to take.

That moment made me flush and nearly swoon with the tingling sense of being wanted. Two men, standing on either side of me as I sat between them, giving them both a good view of my cleavage, and quite a bit of leg as I crossed them, tilting my head back to thank them and laugh at their hungry expressions. Not that it was a laughing matter, but something had to break the tension. Because I was in the middle of two men who were very, deadly serious about getting what they wanted.

"That dress is stunning." Lloyd was the first to move away, probably mindful of his job, especially after our dinner incident the night before. But he was sure to add my name at the end of his compliment, and the sound of it in his mouth made me want to melt. "Charlie. What is that short for? Or is it just a nickname?"

Jack moved to his side of the table, looking between the two of us like a man who'd been wishing for something and wasn't quite sure he really liked it, now that it belonged to him. But he let it happen anyway, even as uncomfortable as it might have been. I think his animal nature, that reptilian part of his brain at the base of his neck, had turned red hot at some point over the weekend, and the temperature just wasn't going to go back down. It was in control, for better or worse, and I was along for the ride.

"Charlene." I smiled up at him—his eyes were dark, darker than I'd seen them, almost the smoky black of his hair, curly and slightly disheveled, as if he'd just rolled out of bed to come to work. Of course, I knew he'd been there all day—since this morning's room service. A long, exhausting day. "You must be tired after working yesterday, and now all day today. Gonna go home tonight and crash?"

He shrugged, his gaze dipping down to my cleavage as I leaned back in the chair, tilting my face up to him, and my breasts as well. There was no doubt in my mind about what I was doing, slowly and deliberately, bit by bit. Seducing him was going to be the easy part, I thought, remembering how he stood hidden by the rubber plant in the corner, cock in hand, watching me orgasm at this very table.

Looking at him, I found my mouth was watering, and I wasn't hungry for food.

"I've got a lot of energy," he replied, flashing me a smile. "Stamina. It's all about stamina."

"I bet you do." I laughed, low and throaty, giving him a wink. "I don't know a woman in the world who doesn't love a man with stamina."

"How about steak?" Jack's voice interrupted us, and I looked over at him, seeing that same look, something caught between pleasure and pain.

"The fish is good tonight, too," Lloyd said, suddenly remembering his job and putting two menus down onto the table. "We've got snapper and salmon."

"Eh. Too light." I shrugged one shoulder, feeling my strap slipping, and letting it go. Both men looked there at the dangling piece of fabric as I opened my menu, pretending to pay attention to it. "I'm hungry for something with a little more…substance." I slid the strap back up slowly over the pale, creamy skin of my shoulder, feeling the heat from their eyes, delighting in it. "Something…meaty."

"Steak should do it, then," Jack countered, not even opening his menu.

I smiled and shrugged. "Maybe."

But Jack ignored my flirty answer, ordering for both of us—no Dom Perignon this time, that was still back in the room, the bottle more than half full—and Lloyd took it all down, promising to be back with our salads and beverages.

"Hey." I touched his knee with mine under the table, getting Jack's attention once Lloyd had departed. It was another slow night in the restaurant, but it was early for dinner—only five. We were mostly alone. "You know I love you."

The words seemed to melt the set to his jaw, and he smiled at me, a more open thing than before, less tight-lipped and stiff. "You sure about that?"

"More sure than I've ever been," I said honestly, and I could tell he saw it in my eyes, that thing we'd been carrying, recreating really, all weekend between us, the life and spark of our marriage and life together, ignited again and burning hot.

"You are something else." His hand moved over my bare knee under the table, sliding my dress aside to seek the heat of my inner thigh and squeezing.

"Are you sure you know what you're doing?" I asked, sipping the water Lloyd had left on the table. Jack's hand slid higher as he leaned forward across the little table, his fingers just reaching the matching red satin panties under the dress.

"Do you trust me?"

"Yes." There was no question, no hesitation. I opened my legs a little, sliding forward in my seat, letting him slip the elastic band aside at my thigh and stroke the hair covering my mound. The sensation set me off, almost purring, like a cat, under his touch.

"Balsamic?" Lloyd was back, holding salads and iced tea on a tray, and Jack sat up, his hand squeezing my leg before making a quick departure from under my dress.

"That was me," I said, pointing to a spot on the table in front of me where he placed the plate. He juggled the rest quite easily, with a swift, fluid grace that stunned me, really. I watched his hands—big hands, strong, the fingers long, though, like someone who played piano or guitar—and couldn't help imagining them touching me like Jack had been a moment before. My belly clenched, released, clenched again, my face flushing, not quite enough to match my dress, but enough to make me reach for water to cool the heat.

The men weren't the only ones full of some sort of unslakable lust tonight.

"Can I get you anything else?" Lloyd asked, looking between us.

I shook my head. "I'm good."

"She is," Jack agreed, dropping me a wink and then glancing up at Lloyd. "How about we add some oysters? A little appetizer?"

"Sure." Lloyd grinned at the obvious inference. "Coming right up."

"You're bad." I rolled my eyes at him when he grinned again, looking pleased with himself, like he was keeping some big secret. "And way too obvious. Who taught you about subtlety? The Jolly Green Giant?"

He chuckled, digging into his salad, but didn't respond. I wasn't that hungry—we'd eaten a big, late breakfast off the silver tray, and had spent the afternoon shopping. Jack had, of course, insisted on buying me yet another expensive dress I thought for sure we couldn't afford, but I'd tried it on and had fallen immediately in love. Not just with the dress, but the look in Jack's eyes when I stepped out of the dressing room wearing it. He looked like he would put a second mortgage on our house just to buy it for me.

And I thought I might let him, just to keep that light right there like that, in his eyes. Smiling, I picked at my salad and drank my water in some small attempt to quench some of the heat burning in my belly. I didn't expect it to work, and it didn't, but it was a distraction, and that was good.

"Here you go." Lloyd was back with the oysters sooner than I'd expected, and Jack plucked one up immediately, sliding it into his mouth and swallowing. I'd never been one for seafood and shuddered as I watched him.

"Try one." Jack looked up at the younger man and nodded at the plate. "They're great for the sex drive. Nature's Viagra."

Lloyd smirked. "I don't think I need one."

"He's got great stamina, remember?" I smiled, nudging Jack under the table.

He winked at me. "So he says."

Lloyd shrugged and didn't jump to defend himself. He was young, but even with his apparent inexperience, he had an air of quiet confidence about him.

Jack slid back another oyster—he was going to finish the whole thing, of course, He knew I wouldn't touch them. "So, Lloyd...I meant to ask you." He took a long drink of water, letting the possibility of a question hang there for a moment. "Did you like the little show my wife put on this afternoon?"

I startled, flushing, and stared at him, aghast. "Jack...oh my god...you...didn't..." The realization of what he'd done—what he must have been talking to Lloyd about in the hotel doorway this morning, just out of earshot—hit me with tremendous force. I could barely breathe.

"Very much." Lloyd's gaze moved to me, and the look in his eyes, that hungry, lustful look, made my knees feel weak. I was glad I was already sitting down.

Jack slid back another oyster and asked, "Want to see the live version?"

I grabbed my water glass, gulping, trying to put out the fire, but it wasn't helping. Not in the least. Both men were driving this train, and I was just along for the ride.

"I'd like to do more than watch." Lloyd's fingers moved over my shoulder, pushing up my errant dress strap, and just the brush of his fingers sent my temperature soaring again.

"Room 431," Jack said matter-of-factly, a clear proposal. "After your shift is over."

"Seven." Lloyd sealed the deal, and they both nodded, coming to an understanding. And I sat there, stunned, thinking vaguely about deals with the devil. Where did the devil really reside, in all of us? I wondered. For me, I knew—where the heat was, emanating fire between my thighs, the place where the world was forged—and the bargain had already been made.

* * * *

There was no small talk, no subtle flirting or seduction. We'd done all that, leading up to the moment, and besides, Jack couldn't wait. He'd started already, and I was wearing just my red silk panties and bra and bent over the edge of the bed within minutes of returning to our room. I'd had an hour, at least, of teasing, and I was on the brink of death-by-pleasure already by the time Lloyd knocked on our hotel room door.

"Jack, wait!" I begged him to let me put something else on. My panties were still in place, although they'd been pulled aside several times, and I currently had the glass dildo shoved deep into my ass, which was sticking up in the air in my position of hands-and-knees on the bed.

"Hey there." Jack ignored my plea, opening the door and letting Lloyd in. He'd changed into jeans and a gray pullover, perhaps even showered—his hair looked slightly damp, from what I could see from my almost upside-down view. Jack was wearing jeans, too, but no shirt. That had disappeared over the course of the hour, along with my bra, probably joining the expensive heap of my dress on the floor.

"Hi." Lloyd's gaze skipped over to me and I flushed at my compromising position, but there was nothing to be done about it. "Looks like you started without me."

"Started," Jack agreed, walking over to the bed and running his hand over my behind, giving the butt plug a little slap and making me jump. "But nowhere near finished."

"Well, that's good." Lloyd came over to the bed but didn't sit on it. He stood beside, looking down at me, and since I was on eye level with his jeans, I could actually watch the bulge there begin to grow. God, that made my mouth water. My pussy was already soaking wet, and I'd been aching to come for…forever.

"Isn't she something?" The pride in Jack's voice was unmistakable, and I flushed at the compliment, sure he meant it that way, but not sure if I should be offended or thrilled. The latter won out as Lloyd nodded, his hand, unconscious and probably involuntary, moving to rub at his crotch. It was probably aching, just like mine was.

"I'll say." The younger man agreed, his thumb moving up and down his zipper line, right where I longed to press my cheek. I wanted to see his cock, close up this time, to touch it and taste it. The fact that my husband had me up on my hands and knees like some offering to another man was like some sublime permission.

I moaned softly when Jack's hands moved over my ass through my panties. I couldn't help arching my back like a cat lifting my behind in the air, wanting more.

"I left the best, last thing for you." Jack snapped the elastic band of my panties. "Go ahead, take them off."

Lloyd looked down at me, his eyes questioning. "Charlie?"

"Yeah," I breathed, nodding, pressing my cheek against the sheet—the comforter was long gone, too, in a wad on the floor on the other side of the bed. "Go ahead."

I couldn't see him then, just feel him, sliding my panties slowly over the rounded swell of my ass, over the dildo pressed deep inside. He stopped there for a moment, his breath catching, before slipping my panties down to my knees.

"A real redhead," Lloyd breathed, close enough to feel the heat of his breath. "What's with the…uh…"

"Bookmark, so to speak." Jack obviously knew what he was talking about, and he chuckled, giving the butt plug a quick twist, making me gasp and moan at the same time. "Holding my place…or yours."

"Oh." Lloyd's voice actually caught when he asked the next question. "Does she like…do you like…?"

"She loves to get her ass fucked." Jack moved the dildo slowly, pulling it back, and I whimpered. "Don't you, baby?"

The ache in my pussy was overriding any possible humiliation. I didn't care anymore, what I had to admit, as long as I got what I wanted.

"Yes," I said, arching, pressing back against the toy, feeling it slipping back into me. "God, yes…"

"You ever fucked a woman in the ass, Lloyd?"

I heard him swallow before he croaked, "No."

"You can touch her," Jack encouraged, and I heard the indulgent smile in his voice. "Go ahead."

A tentative hand moved over my thighs, a finger dipping all too briefly between my pussy lips, making me sigh and wiggle in response. I heard Lloyd's voice, whispering something, but couldn't make out the words. Then there was a tongue probing, parting my flesh, seeking the aching bud of my clit.

"Ohhh!" I moaned as two sets of masculine hands moved me on the bed, flipping me onto my back. Lloyd buried his face between my legs with a groan, spreading my thighs with his palms, and my husband knelt beside me, kneading my breasts, tugging at my nipples, all the while undoing his jeans with the other hand.

The tongue flickering over my clit was practiced and sure, and I closed my eyes in pleasure, my hand moving through the young man's hair, dark and thick and curling around my fingers as I urged him on. It was so strange, so different from Jack's mouth down there, and exciting at the same time.

My eyes flew open when Jack's cock met my lips. In the hour or so of play time we'd had before Lloyd showed up, he hadn't had it out or touched it once. He was like an iron bar sliding into my mouth, the tip slick with precum. I drew him in, eager, using my tongue to tease the head the way I knew he loved. When I glanced down between my thighs, I saw Lloyd's eyes on us, watching me sucking Jack's cock.

I was beyond want—I was all need, rocking my hips up against the mouth working between my legs, my hand pressing the head there hard, my other hand gripping Jack's ass, forcing him deeper into my throat. I gagged, and he thrust deeper anyway, making my eyes water with the force, but I took him, making breathy, choking sounds, feeling my saliva wetting my chin, my cheeks.

When Lloyd began to fuck me with the dildo still stuck in my ass, I went off like someone had turned a switch. I would have screamed if Jack hadn't been buried so tightly into my throat. My pussy spasmed hard and I grabbed Lloyd's hair in my fist, grinding my pussy against his lashing tongue, pressing the toy deeper into my stretched, aching asshole.

"Ohhhh fuck!" I shuddered with my orgasm, managing to disengage from the furious movement of Jack's pumping hips to get the words out. "Oh god, baby, I'm coming so hard!" But Lloyd already knew, his fingers slipping into my clenching pussy as he fucked me with the dildo, his mouth fastened wetly against my mound, not letting me go.

"Oh god, oh god, oh god," I whispered over and over as the sensation peaked and then began to recede in deliciously throbbing waves. I looked down at him, kneeling on the floor next to the bed, his eyes hungry, his face wet with my juices, and I abandoned my husband's cock, sliding down off the bed, too, and kissing Lloyd fully on the mouth.

He groaned, his tongue brushing mine as I tasted my juices, sucking them out of his mouth, pressing my breasts against his chest. His arms went around me, hands gripping my ass, pulling me into his crotch. Jesus, he was hard! My mouth followed my hands as I unbuttoned and unzipped his jeans, sliding them down his hips and urging him onto the bed. He sat on the edge as I explored the newness of his cock with my eyes, my hands, my tongue.

Behind Lloyd, I saw Jack reclining on the bed, his jeans gone now, his hand moving slowly up and down the length of his cock as he watched us. There was no anger or resentment or bitterness in him—just lust, like a dark light turned on behind his eyes. Lloyd's hand moved through my hair as I sucked him harder, feeling him swelling against my tongue. He was just a little smaller than Jack, but the base was thicker, the hair there much darker, and slightly curved as I took him deep into my throat.

Watching Jack stroke himself just made me hungrier for more cock. I reached out a hand to him, never stopping my rhythm, opening and closing my hand, a child's gesture: *want.* He understood, moving beside Lloyd on the bed, and I happily shifted so I was kneeling between the two of them, a cock in each hand. I stroked them in easy rhythm, watching their eyes on me, the red panties gone now, tangled somewhere under Lloyd's clothes on the floor, my breasts swaying gently with the motion.

Lloyd's hand cupped one of them, feeling the weight, thumbing the nipple, making me moan and lean forward to suck the tip of his cock in to my mouth as a reward. He thrust his hips in time with my motion, squeezing my nipple, tugging. I moaned, my hand moving up and down his shaft as I leaned toward Jack, whose hand had moved to my other breast, fondling it gently. I sucked the tip of Jack's cock into my mouth, comparing the two—a little saltier, the head thicker than Lloyd's, the skin not as tight as I stroked him, too.

"I want you," I murmured, sitting back as I stroked them both, tugging on two cocks, my pussy so wet I felt it on my thighs. "Both of you."

It was all the permission they needed. Jack directed, Lloyd on the bed, me on top, straddling him. The younger man's hands moved over my hips, my breasts, as I grabbed his cock, positioning my pussy, aiming him. I hadn't felt anything but my husband's cock inside of me since...my god, when? College. A party, I thought, just after I'd started dating Jack. Some guy at a fraternity party. Fifteen years ago?

"Oh fuck." Lloyd shivered as I slid him inside of me, the sensation of being filled incredible with the dildo still stuck in my ass. His eyes half closed and I leaned down to kiss him, a soft, tender thing. He groaned and wrapped his arms around me, his hips already thrusting. "Oh god, Charlie, you feel so good…"

"So do you," I whispered, grinding my hips, his cock the perfect fit. Jack's hands moved over my ass, and I felt his weight shifting on the bed behind me.

"You ready, baby?" he murmured, pulling on the butt plug. I moaned against Lloyd's mouth, clutching his shoulders as my husband removed the toy from my gaping ass.

"Oh Jack!" I cried, feeling the flesh of his cock pressing against my asshole. I was already lubed up from the toy, but I heard the tell-tale click of the KY anyway.

"Are you okay?" Lloyd's eyes widened as I bit my lip, wincing as Jack grabbed my hips, slowing easing his way into the tight, furrowed passage. It closed up so quickly, became resistant so *fast*.

"He's…" I gasped, moaning as I felt the thickest part of him sliding past that last bit of tightness. "Ohhh god he's fucking my ass."

"Ohhhhhh, fuck," Lloyd said again, grabbing me harder as Jack pressed himself deep into me. "I can feel him…"

I felt them both—the thick length of Jack's cock wedged tightly into my ass, Lloyd's curved arrow buried in my pussy, the two of them separated by a thin wall of flesh, a band of muscle. I squeezed my muscles down there, testing, hearing them both moan with pleasure, and that filled me with lust.

"Fuck me," I urged, beginning to rock, the two of them moving in and out. "Oh yes, fuck me, fuck me!"

"You like those cocks, baby?" Jack asked, thrusting deep. His hands gripped my hips as he rocked, Lloyd's positioned just above his at my waist. The younger man's hips ground upward, burying his cock into the wet crevice there. "You like having two cocks fucking you?"

"Yes!" I moaned, giving in to my own humiliating need, burying my face against Lloyd's neck. "God, yes, yes!"

There was no explaining it, no thinking, there was nothing but pure sensation. I was completely filled with flesh—hard, thrusting, insistent flesh, their hands on me, cocks pounding in rhythm and then out, my whole pelvis buzzing with their lust. I didn't want it to end, ever, and I begged them for more, but it was Jack who gave in first, slowing slightly with a groan.

"Ahhhh fuck, I'm gonna come..."

"Oh on my ass!" I begged, working my hips, making Lloyd moan beneath me. "Come all over me!"

"Ahhhh god, now!" He pulled out so suddenly I whimpered with the loss, but his cock exploded immediately and he pumped it against my asshole, shooting hot jets of his cum between the crack of my ass.

"Oh, wait," Lloyd begged, but I knew there was no stopping him either, feeling his breath hot against my cheek, the fat swell of his cock, and I reached between us, grabbing his cock and sliding up so I could pump him against my clit. "Ohhhh yeah!"

He exploded in my hand, his cum spurting hotly over my clit, making me shiver with pleasure and rub it there, taking me almost immediately over the edge I'd been hovering on. I came, too, climaxing hard, rocking between the hard flesh of both men, their hands still holding me tight.

I couldn't remember much in those first few moments—my ears were still ringing, my breath coming too fast, making the room seem too bright—but they tucked me between them on the bed and I closed my eyes, feeling the long, lean length of them both, a blanket of flesh, and thought with a little regret that I'd never experience anything quite so amazing for the first time again.

My only hope, I decided, snuggled happily, blissfully between them, was that we could do it for the second, or third, or fourth time. That might be good enough solace.

Chapter Nine

I would have thought the morning would bring a measure of awkwardness in the time between impulse and composure, but I woke between the two of them, Jack snoring on my right, his back to my back, and Lloyd already awake, his eyes soft and open, watching me sleep. I didn't even startle, although I was surprised—I hadn't woken up beside anyone besides my husband or children for years—and instead I traced the strong line of his jaw with my thumb, wondering what this young man was going to take away from this capricious sexual encounter. Something to tell college roommates perhaps, regaling them with tales about a chance threesome with a MILF and her husband one weekend.

I knew very well it was nothing more—and the man sleeping behind me was the only one I'd ever want to spend forever with—but there was something youthfully appealing about the other man in my bed, the way he touched me, looked at me. It was so different from Jack, arousingly so, and my body couldn't help but respond.

"He's a lucky man." Lloyd's whispered words made my heart melt, and I kissed him softly as a thank you. Our kiss melted us both together in the early light of dawn, his hands moving over my nude form under the covers, pulling my hips in to meet his. His cock stirred against my thigh, and I couldn't help but remember the times—how many times? Four? Five?—the night before he'd gotten hard, again and again, both of them fucking me in every possible position, from every imaginable angle, until we'd all ended up, sore and exhausted, drinking Dom Perignon and soaking in the big Jacuzzi tub. It was just a brief break, and then we were at it again. I vaguely remembered drifting off.

My head was still a little swimmy, and I couldn't tell if it was because of last night's wine or from Lloyd's hungry, eager kiss. He hadn't been kidding about his stamina, I thought, reaching down to squeeze his swollen flesh in my hand, feeling his hips begin to thrust in response. Behind me, Jack slept on, and I wondered for a moment if he would mind this little secret tryst. Last night, he'd been there, always a presence, but now it was just the two of us while Jack dreamed oblivious beside us, Lloyd pulling me on top of him, suckling my breasts and rubbing his cock up and down between the wet crevice of my pussy.

"Ahhhhh," Lloyd sighed deeply when I slid him inside of me and I pressed my lips to his.

"Shh," I urged, rolling my hips in easy circles, making as little movement on the bed as possible. He caught my rocking rhythm, making almost imperceptible movements around and around, his cock touching my deepest, most secret places. I sat up to straddle him, giving him access to my breasts, and he took advantage of the position, his thumbs working my nipples in the same little circles.

"Mmm." I couldn't help the little noises, soft and breathy, as I rode him faster, a little faster still, my clit aching. I guided his hand down there, and he found my pleasure center soon enough, transferring the circles he'd been making around my nipples to my hungry little clit. God, he was beautiful, long and lean, the muscles in his chest and stomach rippling with every movement. I couldn't stop looking at him, the way his face worked, jaw tightening, releasing, eyes half-closed and sweeping over me as I fucked him.

"Charlie," he whispered, and I slowed, already knowing the signs, just squeezing him with my pussy muscles, making him groan softly.

"Now this is a show worth watching." Jack's voice startled me and I glanced over to see him watching, his eyes dark with lust, his hand wrapped around his cock. "Mind if I tape it for posterity?"

I stared as he got up and opened the laptop sitting on the dresser, the one with the web cam still attached.

"Jack!" I warned, shaking my head. The last thing I wanted was to end up on YouTube—or worse, YouPorn.

"Not live," he assured me, setting the camera up. "Just Memorex. For posterity. You mind, Lloyd?"

"Ahhhh god." Lloyd shifted me on top of him, biting his lip as I wiggled in the saddle of his hips. "No, no, I don't care."

"Turn around, baby," Jack urged, grabbing my hips. I pulled myself off Lloyd's lap reluctantly, turning to straddle him again, glancing over my shoulder to see him smiling up at me. "Smile for the camera."

"Oh stop." I made a face at Jack as he dug into the night table drawer, bringing out the KY. "What are you...?"

But I didn't really have to ask. Jack dribbled a liberal amount of KY over Lloyd's glistening cock—he was plenty wet from my pussy—and then handed me the tube.

"Go ahead."

I rubbed the KY into Lloyd's skin, feeling him respond, swelling, anticipating. He knew where I was going to put it, and he wanted it as much as I did. Then I worked a liberal amount of the gooey stuff slowly around the tight ring of my asshole. You would have thought, after the weekend we'd spent, that it would have a little more give, but the human body is an amazing piece of work. My friend Jodi's comment about it being an "exit only" hole had been, in some ways, right on. That particular orifice would always resist, and I would have to push past that tightness, that control. That was, I thought, part of what made it so appealing.

"Ooooooooooo, wait!" I moaned when Lloyd grabbed and thrust the moment I pressed the head of his cock to the grooved hole of my ass. "Sloooow, baby. Please." He tried, but he was eager, and my ass hadn't been stretched for hours.

"Let me," I murmured, beginning a slow, steady slide, squeezing his cock, holding it even more rigid as I slid the head past the point of no return. We both sighed at that moment, him in pleasure, me in relief, and looking up at Jack, I remember the first time we'd done this together, how scared I'd been, afraid I was going to split apart.

"Nice," Jack remarked, his eyes focused between my legs as I sat fully down on Lloyd's cock, burying him completely in my ass. Jack's cock was hard, back in his hand, and I knew just where he was going to want to put it. I wanted it, too, to be sandwiched between them again, fucked open completely by both of them.

I was still adjusting to feeling of Lloyd's cock, swollen and throbbing in my ass, when Jack moved between my legs, spreading my thighs and aiming his cock for my pussy. Lloyd took my weight as I leaned back, letting Jack slide the length into my cunt. I felt so full I could barely stand it and I whimpered as my husband began to move, thrusting deep and hard, rocking us all on the bed.

"Feels good," Lloyd whispered, his hands moving to cup my breasts. I moaned in response, squeezing my pussy muscles, feeling everything tighten, hugging their cocks. Lloyd swore softly in my ear at the sensation and Jack groaned, slowing for a moment, biting his lip.

"Hold still, baby," Jack whispered, sliding his cock out of me and grabbing the tube of KY. Puzzled, I watched as he lubed himself up, moving back into position between my legs.

"Jack, what are you—?"

"Shh." His cock slipped downward through my pussy, a wet slide, bypassing the entrance and pressing into the tight flesh of my perineum. My eyes flew open wide and I gasped, clutching him as he pressed his weight into me, against both of us, struggling for entrance. He couldn't possibly mean to…

"Jack!" I panted, writhing on top of Lloyd, who was trying to hold me still. "Oh no, Jack, not my ass! You can't put it in my—"

"Holy fuck!" Beneath me, Lloyd's hips bucked, feeling the tightness, the press of Jack's cock against his as they slid together into the channel of my ass. "Oh my god!"

I was already stretched, and couldn't believe I would open any more, but I did, I spread for him, his flesh burning, urgent, his eyes focused on mine. I bit my lip until I thought it would bleed, but I took him, moaning loudly when I felt him slip all the way in, the two of them buried deep in me, beginning to rock, fucking me even more open.

"Ohhhh no," I moaned, shaking my head, feeling Lloyd's lips against my cheek, my hair, whispering soft, unintelligible words. His voice was filled with a tightness, anticipation of what was coming, and I knew it was. Their cocks drove into me, from top and bottom, and I had no choice but to let them, to go along for the ride, my body trapped between two hungry wolves fighting for territory, thrusting me past bliss, past conscious thought, past my own inhibition, taking me so high I wasn't even afraid of heights anymore.

"Ahhhhh fuck!" Lloyd moaned, grabbing my hips, grinding up into my ass. "Ohhh you're gonna make me come."

Jack groaned, too, sliding his cock out of my ass, pulling me forward. Surprised, whimpering at the sudden loss of fullness, I knelt at his instruction, too lost, too gone, to even think as he pressed his cock to my lips. I took him, swallowing the first blast of his cum before Lloyd's cock was there, too, fighting again for position in this orifice, pressing into my mouth, stretching it wide so he, too, could shoot white hot blasts of his cum over my tongue.

"Ohhhh yeah," Jack groaned, grabbing the back of my head. "You nasty, dirty girl. Swallow those cocks!"

I flushed—my whole body flushed—but I did, eager for both of them, swallowing more cum than I thought possible as they wrestled for room. I couldn't possibly take it all and their cum dribbled down my chin, over my breasts, but I licked up as much as I could, running my tongue around the sensitive head of first Lloyd's cock and then Jack's, feeling them both shudder at the intensity of it.

"Your turn," Lloyd said finally, and they both pulled me up, hands under my arms, laying me back on the bed, and I groaned as they jockeyed once again, this time between my thighs, taking turns licking and sucking at my clit.

"Oh yes," I whispered, a hand on each of their heads, wanting more, all of them, all at once. "Oh my god, please, yes, make me come for you!"

Jack moved up to suck at my nipples, and Lloyd fastened his mouth over my clit, lashing his tongue back and forth, sending anticipatory shivers up my spine. I clutched at Jack as I felt my body sailing over the edge, my nails digging into his back, both men working over me, tongues and hands and fingers, and I bucked beneath them, knowing they would hold me, and they did.

My orgasm shook me, shook the bed, left me breathless and panting as both of them moved up to join me, one on either side. Déjà vu, I thought, putting an arm around each. I wanted to stay like that forever—or at least, in this room, with both of them. But I saw Lloyd glance at the clock, and Jack did, too. Checkout was eleven, and while Lloyd had the day off, he would have his real life to return to.

And, so did we. I couldn't imagine trying to integrate the woman I'd become over the weekend, the one who had taken two men into the deepest, most secret parts of her, and the woman I was at "home" in my "real life." The thought of going back to work, making kids' lunches, and giving Jack a cursory kiss goodbye in the morning as we both went off to start our day, was anathema to me.

"I need a shower," I murmured, running my hand through Lloyd's thick curls, my other rubbing the short fuzz at the back of Jack's neck.

"Good idea," Jack agreed, nodding toward the bathroom.

"Definitely." Lloyd sat, reaching for my hand, and so did Jack. I smiled between them, taking one of each, and let them lead me toward the promise of a thorough cleaning.

* * * *

"I don't want to go home."

Everything was packed, all the toys cleaned and put away, the laptop back in its case. And instead of some sexy little dress, I was back into a pair of jeans and a t-shirt, appropriate mommy-wear to go pick up the kids in, curled up on the hotel bed that still smelled like our night and morning-long marathon threesome.

Lloyd was gone—our goodbyes said at the door earlier that morning. He gave us his number, but I knew better. It had been a great night, but that was all. I didn't really believe Jack and I would drift any further into an open marriage than we already had. In fact, once we were back to our little house in the suburbs, I was sure this, all of this would fade like some long ago dream.

"We could stay." Jack smiled, sitting on the bed beside me, brushing hair away from my cheek.

I sighed, sitting up to face him. "No, we can't. The weekend's over."

He chuckled, shaking his head. "Well you don't have to say it like *life's* over or anything."

I looked around the room and sighed. "This one is."

He kissed my cheek, nuzzled my neck. "Poor Charlie. It's always all or nothing, isn't it?"

"Isn't it?" I sighed again, feeling a heaviness in my belly, not knowing how to make it go, but wanting it gone.

"Hey." He tilted my chin up, looking into my eyes. "Do you have any idea how much I love you?"

I smiled, although I felt like crying. "I love you, too."

It was beyond true, no matter what happened, even if this was one shining weekend in the entire lifespan of our marriage to look back on and remember when we were eighty-something. I leaned in and kissed him, hoping we'd both still be around and loving each other this much when we were that old. In spite of who I thought I'd become over the last few weeks, Jack was Jack and always would be. He was the only man I could open up to like I had, the only man who could push me to the edge of wildness and back, the only man I wanted to be with.

"You okay?" He brushed away one of my tears and I smiled through them, not feeling sad anymore.

"Better than okay." I nodded, standing up and holding out my hand. "Let's go home."

Epilogue

"I have a surprise for you."

His words woke me up fully, and I rolled over toward him in bed. The alarm hadn't quite gone off yet—we had ten whole minutes before we had to hit the shower. I couldn't hear the kids up yet. That was a relief. They'd been holy terrors for weeks after we'd returned from our weekend, backlash, I suppose, or payback, maybe. Jack said we needed to go on little vacations more often, to get them used to it. I wholeheartedly agreed, but it had been months and, of course, neither of us had found the time.

"Hmmm, I wonder what surprise that could be," I pondered sleepily, reaching for his cock under the covers, knowing I'd find that morning hard-on and already anticipating it.

"Well, that, yeah." I heard him grinning, but he moved away before I could grasp him. "But something else, too."

"The kids are really quiet," I whispered, glancing up at the ceiling where I usually heard them running around long before the alarm actually went off.

"That's part of the surprise."

I stared at him in the darkness. "What?"

"You're a sound sleeper you know," he said, telling me something we both knew. "I bundled them off to grandma's last night after you went to bed."

"You did not!" I sat up, reaching over and turning on the light, not caring about those last glorious ten minutes anymore. "They're not even home?"

Jack leaned back, his hands laced behind his head, smiling up at me. "She's taking them to school today and keeping them for the weekend." It was Friday, I realized. Thank god, because I was exhausted.

"What are you up to?" The excitement coiled in my belly, and I flashed for a moment on that one amazing weekend. God, it seemed so long ago now...

"Your surprise."

"Every time you say that, I end up—hey! Where are you going?"

"We're calling in to work," Jack said, plucking his laptop off the dresser and bringing it back to bed.

"From your laptop?"

"No." He opened the lid and the screen showed a site called 'The Horny Housewife.' I raised my eyebrows.

"We're staying home to watch porn?"

Jack clicked a link and video opened up. At first I didn't understand, but my body recognized it before my brain did, my pussy and ass clenching as I watched Jack and Lloyd sandwich me between them. Of course, with that black bar across my face, you couldn't tell it was me...

"I thought we'd stay home and *make* porn."

"What is this?" My eyes were glued to the screen, the memory of what was being portrayed there suddenly fresh. "Who is 'The Horny Housewife?'"

"You are."

I stared at him and then looked back at the screen. "Me?"

"Aren't you?" Jack grinned, his eyes lit up like I hadn't seen them in months. I imagined mine were the same as I jumped into his lap, giggling and hugging him.

"You're crazy," I whispered, straddling him, grinding there. "You know that?"

"So let's get crazy together and put on a good show." Jack's hands moved up under my t-shirt, pulling it over my head. I couldn't believe I was going to do this, that I was even thinking about it, and I'd struggled for months to try to bridge the gap between the woman I was during my day-to-day routine and the one I'd glimpsed briefly over that long, blissful weekend.

But this...*The Horny Housewife?* I couldn't help but laugh, and still, I knew it was true. And why not? What was wrong with a little sexual freedom in suburbia, letting your hair down, taking your clothes off, and surrendering to pleasure? Was that so crazy?

"Ready?" Jack nodded toward the camera—he'd obviously set it all up the night before, while I was sleeping, oblivious. I'd never loved him more.

"Of course," I agreed, pushing him back on the bed and climbing him like a tree. "After all, the show must go on."

The End

ABOUT SELENA KITT

Like any feline, Selena Kitt loves the things that make her purr-and wants nothing more than to make others purr right along with her! Pleasure is her middle name, whether it's a short cat nap stretched out in the sun or a long kitty bath. She makes it a priority to explore all the delightful distractions she can find, and follow her vivid and often racy imagination wherever it wants to lead her.

Her writing embodies everything from the spicy to the scandalous, but watch out-this kitty also has sharp claws and her stories often include intriguing edges and twists that take readers to new, thought-provoking depths.

When she's not pawing away at her keyboard, Selena runs an innovative publishing company (www.excessica.com) and in her spare time, she devotes herself to her family—a husband and four children—and her growing organic garden. She also loves bellydancing and photography.

Her books *EcoErotica* (2009), *The Real Mother Goose* (2010) and *Heidi and the Kaiser* (2011) were all Epic Award Finalists. Her only gay male romance, *Second Chance*, won the Epic Award in Erotica in 2011. Her story, *Connections*, was one of the runners-up for the 2006 Rauxa Prize, given annually to an erotic short story of "exceptional literary quality," out of over 1,000 nominees, where awards are judged by a select jury and all entries are read "blind" (without author's name available.)

She can be reached on her website at
www.selenakitt.com

BABYSITTING THE BAUMGARTNERS
By Selena Kitt

Ronnie—or as Mrs. Baumgartner insists on calling her, Veronica—has been babysitting for the Baumgartners since she was fifteen years old and has practically become another member of the family. Now a college freshman, Ronnie jumps at the chance to work on her tan in the Florida Keys with "Doc" and "Mrs. B" under the pretense of babysitting the kids. Ronnie isn't the only one with ulterior motives, though, and she discovers that the Baumgartners have wayward plans for their young babysitter. This wicked hot sun and sand coming of age story will seduce you as quickly as the Baumgartners seduce innocent Ronnie and leave everyone yearning for more!

Warning: This title contains MFF threesome, lesbian, and anal sex.

EXCERPT from
BABYSITTING THE BAUMGARTNERS:

When my legs felt steady enough to hold me, I got out of the shower and dried off, wrapping myself in one of the big white bath sheets. My room was across the hall from the bathroom, and the Baumgartner's was the next room over. The kids' rooms were at the other end of the hallway.

As I made my way across the hall, I heard Mrs. B's voice from behind their door. "You want that tight little nineteen-year-old pussy, Doc?"

I stopped, my heart leaping, my breath caught. *Oh my God.* Were they talking about me? He said something, but it was low, and I couldn't quite make it out. Then she said, "Just wait until I wax it for you. It'll be soft and smooth as a baby."

Shocked, I reached down between my legs, cupping my pussy as if to protect it, standing there transfixed, listening. I stepped closer to their door, seeing it wasn't completely closed, still trying to hear what they were saying. There wasn't any noise, now.

"Oh God!" I heard him groan. "Suck it harder."

My eyes wide, I felt the pulse returning between my thighs, a slow, steady heat. Was she sucking his cock? I remembered what it looked like in his hand--even from a distance, I could tell it was big--much bigger than any of the boys I'd ever been with.

"Ahhhh fuck, Carrie!" He moaned. I bit my lip, hearing Mrs. B's first name felt so wrong, somehow. "Take it all, baby!"

All?! My jaw dropped as I tried to imagine, pressing my hand over my throbbing mound. Mrs. B said something, but I couldn't hear it, and as I leaned toward the door, I bumped it with the towel wrapped around my hair. My hand went to my mouth and I took an involuntary step back as the door edged open just a crack. I turned to go to my room, but I knew that they would hear the sound of my door.

"You want to fuck me, baby?" she purred. "God, I'm so wet ... did you see her sweet little tits?"

"Fuck, yeah," he murmured. "I wanted to come all over them."

Hearing his voice, I stepped back toward the door, peering through the crack. The bed was behind the door, at the opposite angle, but there was a large vanity table and mirror against the other wall, and I could see them reflected in it. Mrs. B was completely naked, kneeling over him. I saw her face, her breasts swinging as she took him into her mouth. His cock stood straight up in the air.

"She's got beautiful tits, doesn't she?" Mrs. B ran her tongue up and down the shaft.

"Yeah." His hand moved in her hair, pressing her down onto his cock. "I want to see her little pussy so bad. God, she's so beautiful."

"Do you want to see me eat it?" She moved up onto him, still stroking his cock. "Do you want to watch me lick that sweet, shaved cunt?"

I pressed a cool palm to my flushed cheek, but my other hand rubbed the towel between my legs as I watched. I'd never heard anyone say that word out loud and it both shocked and excited me.

"Oh God, yeah!" He grabbed her tits as they swayed over him. I saw her riding him, and knew he must be inside of her. "I want inside her tight little cunt."

I moved the towel aside and slipped my fingers between my lips.

He's talking about me!

The thought made my whole body tingle, and my pussy felt on fire. Already slick and wet from my orgasm in the shower, my fingers slid easily through my slit.

"I want to fuck her while she eats your pussy." He thrust up into her, his hands gripping her hips. Her breasts swayed as they rocked together. My eyes widened at the image he conjured, but Mrs. B moaned, moving faster on top of him.

"Yeah, baby!" She leaned over, her breasts dangling in his face. His hands went to them, his mouth sucking at her nipples, making her squeal and slam down against him even harder. "You want her on her hands and knees, her tight little ass in the air?"

He groaned, and I rubbed my clit even faster as he grabbed her and practically threw her off him onto the bed. She seemed to know what he wanted, because she got onto her hands and knees and he fucked her like that, from behind. The sound of them, flesh slapping against flesh, filled the room.

They were turned toward the mirror, but Mrs. B had her face buried in her arms, her ass lifted high in the air. Doc's eyes looked down between their legs, like he was watching himself slide in and out of her.

"Fuck!" Mrs. B's voice was muffled. "Oh fuck, Doc! Make me come!"

He grunted and drove into her harder. I watched her shudder and grab the covers in her fists. He didn't stop, though--his hands grabbed her hips and he worked himself into her over and over. I felt weak-kneed and full of heat, my fingers rubbing my aching clit in fast little circles. Mrs. B's orgasm had almost sent me right over the edge. I was very, very close.

"That tight nineteen-year-old cunt!" He shoved into her. "I want to taste her." He slammed into her again.

"Fuck her." And again. "Make her come." And again. "Make her scream until she can't take anymore."

I leaned my forehead against the doorjamb for support, trying to control how fast my breath was coming, how fast my climax was coming, but I couldn't. I whimpered, watching him fuck her and knowing he was imagining me ... *me!*

"Come here." He pulled out and Mrs. B turned around like she knew what he wanted. "Swallow it."

He knelt up on the bed as she pumped and sucked at his cock. I saw the first spurt land against her cheek, a thick white strand of cum, and then she covered the head with her mouth and swallowed, making soft mewing noises in her throat. I came then, too, shuddering and shivering against the doorframe, biting my lip to keep from crying out.

When I opened my eyes and came to my senses, Mrs. B was still on her hands and knees, focused between his legs--but Doc was looking right at me, his dark eyes on mine.

He saw me. For the second time today--he saw me.

My hand flew to my mouth and I stumbled back, fumbling for the doorknob behind me I knew was there. I finally found it, slipping into my room and shutting the door behind me. I leaned against it, my heart pounding, my pussy dripping, and wondered what I was going to do now.

YOU'VE REACHED "THE END!"

BUY THIS AND MORE TITLES AT www.eXcessica.com

eXcessica's **YAHOO GROUP**
groups.yahoo.com/group/eXcessica/

Check us out for updates about eXcessica books!

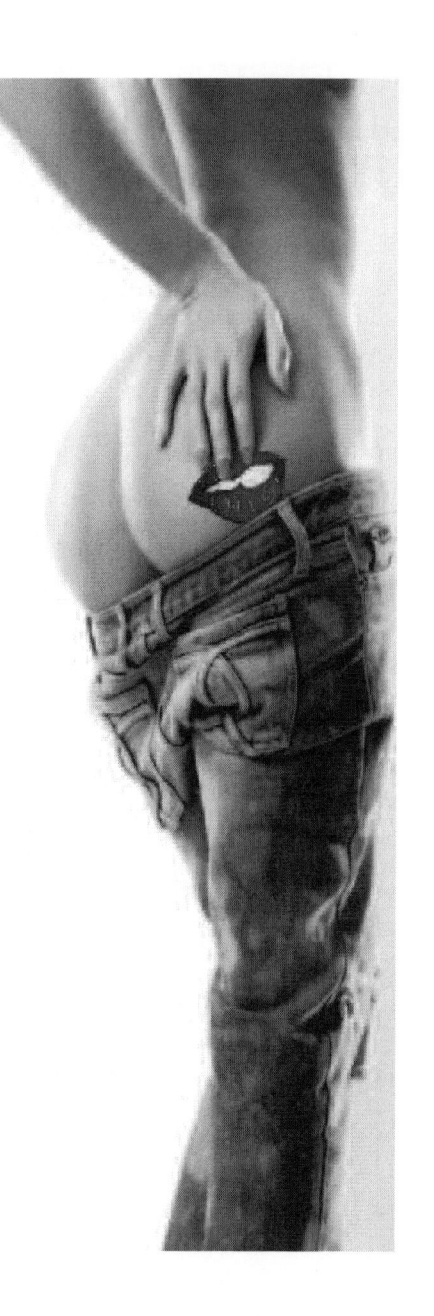

Printed in Poland
by Amazon Fulfillment
Poland Sp. z o.o., Wrocław